THE NUCLEUS OF REALITY

OR THE RECOLLECTIONS OF THOMAS P-

L. A. DAVENPORT

P-WAVE PRESS

To R—, wherever you are.

PREFACE

Thomas P— and I were friends for a long time. I say 'were' because, although he is still alive and apparently well, the Thomas I knew and cared for is long gone.

The last time I saw him as I like to remember him was maybe ten years ago, in a pub we had been going to with a friend ever since we'd met. We both saw Thomas was agitated, but for the most part he was his normal self, mocking us for settling down, taking us on amusing flights of fancy and making acute observations about everyone who caught his eye.

Yet it was clear something was wrong, that maybe he was pushing himself too hard. It was understandable, after all he had been through, to want to throw himself into his job, but we wanted him to see it was okay to slow down and start afresh. We parted that evening with a plan we would meet again soon but he cancelled and I never saw him again.

Yet I did see him again, in a literal sense. It was maybe a year later, and we passed each other in the street. I was on the other side of town for a meeting. I didn't remember Thomas had a place there and I was surprised to see him walking towards me.

But it wasn't him. Not the Thomas I knew. He was bedraggled and vacant, haunted even. He barely recognised me, and when he did, he told me he was involved in something incredibly important and had to go. I watched him hurry off, and that was the last I saw of him.

I would think about him from time to time, especially when I talking with my children. Thomas and I always imagined he would be like an uncle to my children. He was even godfather to my eldest boy.

And then, a few months ago, an envelope turned up from an institution on the other side of the country. Puzzled, I opened it up to find a pile of numbered typewritten pages in a folder. An accompanying letter said Thomas wanted me to have it. I was to do with it as I wished, but he hoped it would help me understand.

I was so surprised to hear from him, even indirectly, I didn't know what to think. I was sad things hadn't turned out how we had all hoped, but it was a relief to know he was being taken care of.

It was hard reading what he had written, and some of it will seem bizarre or even ridiculous. But if I have understood anything from what he says, it is that we should try to see the things that are valuable and beautiful in our life before they are gone.

I also believe Thomas wants others to learn from his experiences. So, after much discussion with my family and the friend with whom we passed so many evenings together, I decided to present it to the world. I should note, while the subtitle of the book is Thomas's own, I devised the title. Although it is hard at times to say what is fact and what is the fanciful invention of Thomas's imagination, it is all true to him. And that, I think, is all we can hope for.

L A Davenport, 2020

ONE

IT STARTED WHEN I JOINED THE QUEUE TO BE SEATED IN ONE of those Japanese chains you see everywhere nowadays. You know the kind. All long beige benches and wipe-clean tables. An open kitchen and quick turnarounds.

I can't remember exactly what town it was in. I must have travelled for work three or four times in as many weeks and they'd all blurred into one.

The restaurant was in one of those redeveloped areas that spring up all the time in European cities. You'll have seen them a hundred times. Two giant office blocks in glass and metal next to each other in what used to be a dock or maybe a collection of factories. Before all the work went to China and they burned the fossil fuels on our behalf so we might have clean air.

In the windy ravine between the two buildings, the developers always keep a cog or two from a giant machine, embed it in concrete and call it Art. And then they put in the same restaurants and shops as you find everywhere else. The same places to eat, the same places to shop. No wonder I can't remember where I was.

So there I stood, at the back of the queue, hovering near the door. I knew I should really go back to my hotel room and finish my presentation for the next day. With all the travelling and the crisis back at the office I'd had to sort out remotely, I hadn't had time to even think about it. But I also knew I needed to eat.

I'd missed lunch, what with all the taxis, trains, security checks, endless queues, then working on the flight, before more endless queues, security checks, trains and taxis. I was hungry. And my head swam with exhaustion.

I stared at the back of the head of the man in front of me, at his neat hair and neat bald patch. He had on an urban combat jacket, as if he was on his way to join a protest movement and had stopped off for a quick bite to eat. But his neat hair gave him away. That and his clean fingernails, which I saw when he answered his phone. He wasn't a protestor, just a dreamer.

I didn't want to listen in on his call, so I stared out of the window. No, correction: I stared *at* the window. The lights and the people reflected in the glass danced and flowed in a colourful mass smeared across the surface, and I watched its slow transformation. Person, shadow, reflection, light, all merging into one, separating, swirling in a ballet of light.

Then I saw the dirt marks on the pane of glass, and the restaurant and the tiredness came back to me in a flood. I was dizzy and nauseous and had to steady myself on the low wall separating the entrance from the diners beyond.

I glanced around to distract myself. The place was full, and noisy. I hadn't really noticed before, but it was all a little overwhelming. I wondered if I could handle staying there and eating.

I blinked and stared ahead. The man with the neat hair and neat bald patch was almost at the front of the queue. I glanced round again and saw other would-be diners had come in and were waiting patiently behind me for me to move forward, closer to Neat Hair.

Now, this next part is very important, if you are to understand the rest of what I am going to tell you. It was the first time, the very first moment, I realised something was wrong. Terribly wrong. But bear with me, as it's necessary for me to get all the details right if I am to explain myself.

What I remember is the man in front of me in the queue was taken away by a waitress and led into the far corner of the restaurant, where he disappeared from view. To be honest, I hadn't given him another thought until I started writing this, so we can probably forget about him.

Then, the waitress came back and I thought she would take me to my seat. But she grabbed a menu and walked along the other side of the low wall, presumably to a customer who was already seated. As she walked away, I followed her with my eyes, noticing her half-dyed light-brown hair, which was tied loosely back in several places. I noticed her freckled skin, the way she leaned forward over her toes as she walked, the texture of the dark khaki shirt she wore under her uniform, and how it puffed out in several places from her constant movement.

I also noticed she was small. Consequently, my eye line was level with the faces of the people sitting at the nearest row of benches. And as the waitress disappeared from view, I naturally scanned the diners in my line of sight as I returned to face the front and wait my turn.

As I reached the last group of customers, my heart stopped.

There, sitting on the corner of the last bench, lost in conversation with her fellow diners, was a young woman who looked identical to a friend of mine. But she didn't look as my friend might look today; rather, exactly as she was twenty years ago, when we first started working together, when we were starting out in our careers and enjoying the spoils of city life.

When I say 'identical', I mean identical. She was *exactly the same* as my friend had been all those years ago. It was remarkable. Even now, thinking back to it, back to her in that moment, I get shivers down my spine.

And it wasn't just her face, which was constructed in precisely the same manner, with the delicate jut of her chin, her high cheekbones, her big, dark eyes, her pale complexion and a shock of black-brown hair swept back in precisely the same way Lucy had worn it all those years ago.

It wasn't just that, although that would have been enough to give me a shock. No, she not only looked exactly the same, but had exactly the same expressions, exactly the same mannerisms, exactly the same laugh as Lucy. It was so striking, it made my head spin and I was overwhelmed. I wanted to turn away, to grab something to hold on to, to sit down. I became faint. I wanted to run out of the door and keep on running until I couldn't anymore.

And then something extraordinary happened.

She glanced over her shoulder and my breath caught in my chest. I reeled in shock, but I couldn't stop staring at her. There was no doubt anymore. This wasn't someone who looked like Lucy. It *was* Lucy. Exactly as she was twenty years ago. I didn't care how this could be, how this could possibly have happened, but there she was, my Lucy, from all those years ago, right in front of me.

Then she turned towards me and our eyes locked. My stomach dropped and a tight band wrapped around my chest. I was no longer aware of anything. All was silent. She did nothing, her expression remained the same. She said nothing. She simply stared at me, her eyes boring into my soul, my past, every moment we had shared filled my mind, and I ached to be back there.

She looked away and so did I. I had to. I turned and stared out of the window. It was no longer a ballet of light and shadow, but people walking along a windswept ravine walled in glass and metal, cold and hard in the coming night. My mind was racing and I had an out-of-body experience, seeing myself waiting in the queue, staring out of the window.

But wait.

We were not home, Lucy and I. No. This was not the city where we knew each other. I had been going there for a long time, but I've never lived there, and neither had she. We'd known each other in another life, not this one. Come to think of it, we hadn't seen each other for… well, a very long time. So what was she doing there?

No, no, don't be silly. That isn't her. That's not her from twenty years ago, when you were both, what? Twenty-two, twenty-three? You don't even know what she would look like now, all these years later.

But wait.

Didn't she… didn't she just laugh exactly like Lucy did?

No, it's not possible. You must be mistaken. That's it. You're mistaken. It's all that tiredness and the travel. It can't be her. Just forget about it.

I shook my head to free myself from the thought and stared hard at the street outside.

But what if…? After all, you've seen her somewhere else, haven't you? You know you have. On another trip, last year. Where was it? Somewhere in Germany? It can't have been Frankfurt, can it? You saw her through the window of a bookshop. It was so uncanny you stopped and stared at her, standing there in the middle of the street like a stalker. You went inside the shop, didn't you, and stood staring at her.

You weren't so sure it was her, though. Not as sure as you are now.

She was alone then, in Germany, browsing for books. Not like now, laughing and joking with her friends, not simply looking like her, but actually being her. And haven't you seen other people from the past? Here and there, in crowds, in markets, in concert halls? What about that time at the photography exhibition?

Yes, yes, but this time is different. She doesn't simply look like her. She *is* her.

I turned back to take another look but my heart jumped into my mouth when I saw she was gone. And her friends too. The waitress was clearing up their places. They must have paid and left. It was not as if she had gone to the toilets, otherwise the others would be waiting for her. But where was she? If she'd settled up and left, then she and her friends would have had to have passed me to leave the restaurant.

I looked around in a panic. There was no sign of them. Nothing. But how? There was no other door, no other way of leaving. They must have passed me to leave. So where were they now?

The waitress arrived and stood in front of me, smiling. She grabbed a menu and I stared at her, unable to comprehend what she was doing.

— Your table is ready. If you would like to follow me.

These were the first words anyone had addressed to me since I'd checked into my hotel earlier that afternoon. They snapped me out of my reverie. I looked at her, and then turned and ran out of the restaurant, pulling frantically at the metal door handle and barging past a middle-aged couple clearly on their way to, or from, a well-to-do gathering.

I stood in the middle of the windy ravine and looked up and down the street, desperately searching every face and silhouette I could see. Even if they had managed to pass me on their way to the door without me spotting them, I had no idea which way they would go.

In one direction lay the metro station and more shops and restaurants; in the other, a park and residential streets. I looked up and down the street again, unsure what to do, my feet rooted to the spot. I stared straight ahead and noticed for the first time a supermarket in the basement of the office block in front of me. Running along the windows, searching the faces of the shoppers below me, I saw no one I recognised.

I turned away and looked up at the sky. It was night-time, but the clouds reflected the bright white and yellow of the city lights. It was cold. I hadn't noticed before. I looked down at the ground. In between the paving stones were thin metal lines. I wondered what they meant, those lines, and where they were going.

Probably nowhere.

The restaurant seemed bright and cosy from this distance. I could see the middle-aged couple were near the front of the queue now. She was wearing an evening dress with a large shawl, all in black, him in a dinner jacket. Her hair was black. He had his black back to me. He stooped as he lifted the black shawl from her black shoulders, folded it and laid it neatly over his black arm.

I wondered what their home was like, what they were talking about, where they had been that evening.

And then I walked away.

TWO

It happened again. It was a different trip to a different city and a couple of weeks later. I can't say I was expecting it, but the first experience had, if I am being honest, never left my mind. I hadn't specifically thought about it, not consciously. But it had been there, floating in the background.

Actually, I did think about it again when I was waiting in the queue to get on a flight. I travelled so much during that period I can't quite recall which airport it was or where I was going. But I clearly remember standing waiting on the jet bridge or whatever they call that tube of metal and glass you have to walk down to get on the plane.

It was sunny outside and quite hot, and the temperature in this metal and glass tube soon became unbearable. I don't know why we were waiting for so long. There seemed to be nothing happening. I'd been late for the plane, at least by my standards, and so was halfway along the queue to board, rather than at the front, stuck at the point where the tube turned and descended towards the door of the plane.

Right in front of me was a German family. Dad and Mum

were in their late forties or early fifties, I suppose, and they looked well preserved. The kids were already in their late teens. Of course they were bored, the young ones. We all were. We older ones just hid it better.

The older child, a boy with foppish hair and the curved stance of someone self-consciously tall, looked up and down the queue. I watched him surreptitiously and inadvertently caught his eye as he scanned past my face. We smiled at each other in that 'isn't this all very dull?' way. His mother must have seen me because she shot me a glance so serious and challenging I had to smile back as sweetly as I could.

I won't touch your baby, I'm not like that.

She smiled and turned away to talk to her husband for want of something else to do, and there was something in her look, in the structure of her face, the way she had her hands half thrust into the back pockets of her jeans, that took me straight back to the restaurant queue, Lucy and the feeling that gripped me by the throat and ripped me inside out. She didn't really look like Lucy, but something about her switched on that memory.

Then the queue for the plane started moving and my mind drifted to her daughter's shoes, the patina on the carpet, the sunshine beating down through the glass and the airport truck driving by underneath our jet bridge, dragging two trailers full of suitcases on their way to somewhere else.

ANOTHER TIME, another airport, another year. It was raining hard and everything was reflected in grey light. I was on one of those buses that take you from the terminal to the plane, standing right at the back next to a woman I didn't know, looking out at the rain-sodden airport, the shiny tarmac. I was happy to be leaving and going anywhere else.

On and on we drove from the gate, snaking along the wet

roadways, seemingly driving in a circle around the terminal building, criss-crossing other roadways and passing other buses, trucks, vans and fuel tankers. At one intersection, a truck drawing two trailers of suitcases swung around behind us on the way to a plane in the opposite direction. The suitcases were uncovered and I thought about them getting wet, the clothes inside being damaged.

As we were about to lose sight of the trailers, the truck took a sharp turn and one of the suitcases tipped and fell off the trailer, reeling on the wet tarmac, lost and alone. The woman I didn't know looked at me and I looked back at her, both in shock, both with our mouths open, knowing exactly what the other was thinking without having to say anything.

THE NEXT TIME IT HAPPENED, I was in another restaurant in another city. It was another time altogether. I don't remember where I was, neither the city nor the restaurant, although I remember it was a pizza place. Wanting the sharp taste of good tomato sauce on a well-cooked base, I had spent some time alone in my room, searching online for the best place in town. I was excited as I stood in the queue, watching the buzz of a restaurant full of people who wanted to be there, to eat that food, now. Everyone seemingly happy and glad to be alive.

If only I could remember where it was.

I seem to recall... No. I don't know why I would have been there, in that city. It must have been for a client meeting because I can still smell the fusty meeting room where we sat cooped up for most of the day. I remember the slippery carpet squares beneath my feet as I walked down the corridor, and the bad coffee from the large pots that were brought up every now and again.

We stopped for lunch.

. . .

THERE IS the canteen downstairs in the office, and there you are, sandwich in hand, the forced smile creeping up your face as you laugh at a joke you don't find amusing with a client who acts as if he's a modern man with feelings, but really he's just a sexist bigot who talks over people until he gets what he wants. No amount of trendy glasses and open-collar shirts will hide your nascent anger, mister. But you swallow it all down with the indifferent sandwiches and more bad coffee.

That's what we agreed, right? When we were in the office before I went on the trip, and I was complaining about his attitude?

He is paying the bills, so we have to suck up a bit of his crap every now and again. No more saying what you think. We agreed. We all think these things, and the clients know we think these things, but they get off on being able to act like a dick because they know we can't say anything. We just have to deal with it. And no, we cannot choose our clients, much as we'd like to.

SO THERE I WAS, at the meeting. I kept my mouth shut and everything was hunky dory. And as I ate my sandwich and laughed at the client's jokes and drank their coffee, and I decided I would reward myself for my good behaviour with the best pizza in town. I hadn't asked them for a recommendation because I was afraid they would suggest we ate together, so I said I needed to work at the hotel and we'd do it next time.

And there I lay on my bed, with my complimentary towels and the remote control beside me, and the view out over the old industrial zone, with its shiny new office blocks in glass and metal, and its identical restaurants and bars down at the bottom of the windy ravine. And I searched and searched and searched until I found *the* place. The place with the best pizza in town.

They said they get their flour all the way from Italy and their tomatoes from Naples and all the rest, but a guy from Calabria who runs a small deli I used to frequent when I first moved to the city told me it's the Italian water that makes all the difference to the taste, not the ingredients. The water there is light and sweet. He told me that one day when I was marvelling at how coffee here never tastes as good as it does over there.

So I stood in the queue for the restaurant, happy, excited even. The day had gone well enough and I was content to be alone, able to watch the world and observe from my little corner, disturbing no one and no one disturbing me.

Apart from the waitress, of course. But she was not disturbing me, not really. She, the waitress, was tall, the tallest waitress here in this Italian pizza place far from Italy. Her dark hair was dyed blonde and purple and red, and tied back. She had elaborate multicoloured tattoos all up both arms, over her neck and disappearing into her strappy top. She walked with quick precision, a mixture of grace and efficiency, and had an otherworldly beauty. It seemed as if the management had persuaded a magnificent parrot from the Amazon rainforest to serve their customers.

I watched her flitting back and forth and smiled. Then I glanced along the tables and benches, full of people talking, laughing, eating, drinking, all absorbed in their personal universe.

And then my stomach dropped out of my personal universe. I closed my eyes for a second, and then reopened them. I was afraid... yes, there she was, just as she had been in the Japanese restaurant. I don't know if she was with the same people as she had been last time, but it was her, her, her. Just as she was twenty years ago, just as she had been a few weeks before. She smiled and laughed and I was lifted back into that space where we lived together all that time ago. It *was* her. And my heart sang.

I wasn't going to make the same mistake this time, so I stepped forward to speak to her.

— Your table is ready. If you'd like to follow me.

I stepped back and, jolted out of the moment, blinked in confusion at the magnificent parrot.

— What? Sorry, what did you say?

— Your table is ready.

I thanked her and turned back to try to catch Lucy's attention. But she was gone. Her table was empty. She was not there, and neither were her friends. The table had been cleared and was ready for the next customers.

How could that be?

— Excuse me, I heard myself stammer.

— Yes? replied the magnificent parrot, inclining her head and shaking her hair slightly.

— That table there... I pointed to where Lucy had been. — Where did they go?

— What do you mean?

— Just a second ago, there were people sitting at that table. A young woman and her friends. And now they are gone. Where did they go?

The magnificent parrot looked at where I was pointing, following the line of my finger with her glass dark eyes.

— There was no one there. That table is reserved. We're waiting for the party to arrive.

I stared at her, my mind swimming and barely able to understand what she could possibly be saying to me. I was faint and dizzy, and nausea swept up through me. Swallowing hard, I stared into her glass dark eyes to see if she was playing a joke on me.

— Are you okay? she said, reaching out her hand towards me.

I stared at her hand and watched in disbelief as feathers, one or two at first, and then hundreds, spouted all along her fingers, and then up her arms. Thick, iridescent black feathers, shining and glowing in purple and red as her arm turned in the light.

I looked up at her face and saw it was covered in the same iridescent black feathers, and she gazed at me with glass dark eyes, blinking briefly. As she shook her head, her feathers shook, and a smile played around her large hooked beak.

— I… I…

I glanced around the restaurant. The diners were all still there, but there was no sound. My throat was thick and heavy and I could barely breathe. I turned and ran out into the fresh air, and vomited into the gutter.

A homeless man sitting by the door of the restaurant asked me if I was okay with a kindness I didn't deserve. I tried to smile at him, but I clearly didn't manage it as he looked horrified.

I stumbled up the road towards the main square of the city and the bustle of people and lights, wanting to lose myself in the crowd, not to think about it anymore.

And then I remembered I still hadn't eaten my pizza.

THREE

I USED TO BE GOOD AT MY JOB.

At some point.

I'm not just saying that. I'm not being arrogant. I *was* good at my job. So good they wanted me to stop doing it so I could manage other people doing it less well than me. They told me, time after time, how good I was at my job, and then I was running a team and reporting to directors and not doing it anymore. And then I was teaching people and giving lectures and travelling the world to talk about my job and be an expert on something I didn't do and probably couldn't do anymore.

All those conferences, all those presentations. A member of the committee shaking my hand and thanking me for coming and saying we're ready for you over here. Slide sets and a microphone. A laser pointer and jokes on repeat. Audiences, some interested, some bored, some asleep.

Then there were the client meetings and the lying. Not outright lies, of course, but glossing, making things shiny to win business and we'll work out the rest later. And I still wasn't doing my job, not the one I did originally, not the one

I liked and wanted to do when I applied to the company in the first place.

There I would sit, encouraging younger versions of myself to believe there was something for them if they developed and grew and got better. Managing their expectations, and their disappointments, slight and occasional at the beginning until it dawned on them they had been strung along. And then the choice: to stay and fight for something that might or might not come along somewhere down the line, or cut your losses and see if the grass really is greener on the other side.

Or maybe it'll be the same old bullshit and lies packaged as opportunities in name only.

OF COURSE, I fought for them, my team, badgering the directors for more money, more responsibility, more hope. As soon as we win this next client, as soon as the next project is complete, we'll sit down and work something out. But it never materialised and I knew I'd have to repeat the same old lies until those bright young things gave up and left.

Those were the good ones, the ones who left. The lazy ones didn't go when they realised they were being exploited. Instead, they would gradually sink under the pressure until there was nothing left and they became shells of their former selves, continuing by the force of some perpetual motion, fuelled by financial obligations and a sense of duty.

Why did I stay? How did I end up becoming their manager, taking every opportunity to travel so I could never stand still long enough to look at myself in the mirror?

Good question.

. . .

I TOLD SOMEONE, you know. About seeing Lucy, I mean. It was after the incident in the Japanese restaurant. I still had a couple of friends at that time. From way back. We'd meet every now and again and have a drink in a bar, usually straight after work, talking about this and that and whatever we had been up to lately.

When we first knew each other, the three of us would meet straight after work and stand there in a little circle. Or maybe it was a triangle. We'd stand there and talk and talk and talk, with our bags on the floor between our feet, until it was closing time, eating packets of nuts and crisps and drinking endless pints, not going anywhere to dine, not even sitting down.

We were excited by everything, but mostly by life and what we thought, or hoped, it had to offer. I liked that time because we didn't know what we would end up doing with our lives. The possibilities seemed limitless.

In reality, the possibilities were limited to a series of binary choices, with the obligations of money hemming even those in to a highly restricted set of options.

I don't remember which one of them caved first, but in the end both of them were married, had a mortgage, and then two children each. I say 'caved' as if it was inevitable they should do those things and those choices represented some kind of defeat. How can it be a defeat to do the same things the vast majority of people have been doing since the dawn of human history? Or at least settled urban history, which is indeed most of human history.

Like it or not, there is an expected life path set out by society and culture for the average individual. And there isn't much outside of that which doesn't lead to disapprobation, pity or some sort of sadness from people who assume you never managed to get it together enough to settle down, and your life must therefore be empty.

. . .

MY LIFE WAS EMPTY. I see that now.

It had been for a long time.

MANY YEARS AGO, and without really thinking too much about it, I had tried to fill the hole in the way society prescribes and got married. She was a nice person, a good person, and she cared for me and I for her. But I was empty and struggling even to be a hollow person, and being married only threw that into the sharpest relief.

A married man.

It seems strange to say that.

A married man.

Marriage was a coat that belonged on someone else's shoulders. It never suited or even fitted me. After a while, she told me she didn't want children, and I saw that was the false war we were supposed to fight to justify our separation. I drifted back into the empty space I had been in since I was a teenager and we parted.

We said we were sad and I at least cried. She did not and the divorce was a formality. There had apparently been an unexpressed ending to the sentence when she told me she didn't want children, as she met someone three months after the divorce, got pregnant, got married and had quite the brood.

And the emptiness was still there. It was a hole that had been cut out of me. A hole that would fill up every day, like a well, brimming with sparkling shadows and reflections. I would sit and stare into the dark water and be lost, trapped in an infinite nothingness. In the morning, the hole would be empty, then slowly it would refill, and we would start the whole process again.

. . .

'WE'? Who is the 'we' who would start the whole process again the next day? Why, me and my other self, of course. The other self who kept me company in my loneliness. Maybe it was he who cut out the hole in me.

I MOVED into a small apartment on the other side of the city. I took my stuff with me, and when it was all unpacked, in that much smaller space, I saw we, my wife and I, had made a home and I hadn't noticed. I had been a lodger in our life, a husband in name only, present but as an actor, playing a role and speaking the lines of someone who appeared to feel and connect, but didn't know what the words meant.

I cared for her deeply and I loved her. That is what I have to believe and it is what I told myself, and her. But if love existed, it was all so deep inside, buried beneath so much weight, I could never bring it up to the surface. I could therefore never show it to her, and so of course she never felt it.

There was nothing in the empty space between us, even though I never forgot her birthday, and I held her warm, soft hand when we walked down the street, and I laughed at her friend's jokes, and I told her I liked the pictures she put up on the wall, and I gave her a massage at least once a month, and I sat in silence, stroking her ankles while she stretched out on the sofa and watched romantic comedies, and I went on holiday with her to wherever she wanted to go, and we kissed with tongues from time to time, and we had sex every couple of weeks, and I knew when she was getting her period, and I made her parents think she'd made a good choice in marrying me, and I held her and rocked her to sleep when her grandma died.

I did all of those things and more, but they meant

nothing because I wasn't present. I didn't make her feel I loved her. She once told me she'd had the realisation, when she was doing the washing up and waiting for me to come home, it could all end and it wouldn't matter to me; I would just find someone else, move in with them and carry on with my life.

What she meant was she thought, to me, she was interchangeable; it didn't matter who I was with; it was all the same to me.

But then we divorced and she met someone else, moved in with them and carried on with life. And I realised one day, when I was doing the washing up and looking out of the kitchen window and listening to the brittle clatter of the plates, that although she hadn't seen it at the time, she had been talking about herself.

She was afraid it would all end and I wouldn't matter to *her*, and she knew *she* was the one who could move on and find someone else. She hadn't wanted to admit to herself she was that kind of person, so she projected it on to me.

I had been going through the motions, and it turned out, so had she. I had been living without thinking, a passenger in my own life. And so had she; she just didn't want to be with someone else who was like that.

And it was I who was left alone, trapped inside my body, an empty well filling up every day with dark water, brimming with reflections.

WHEN I MET up with my friends after I saw Lucy in the Japanese restaurant, they told me they couldn't stay long because they had to get home and help their wives put the kids to bed. The dark water rose up inside me and another self, who was so much more worldly than me and always knew the right things to say (how I wish he'd been in charge in some of the more opportune moments of my life), whispered to me I should tell them about having seen Lucy.

So I started speaking. They were patient and kind and heard me out. I wondered if, maybe, they were taking me seriously and I wasn't going mad after all. But when I got to the end of the story, one of them told me I think too much and needed to spend less time travelling. He said I needed some roots and to start having a life again. I needed to move on from the divorce and all the pain it had caused me.

The other friend agreed. He said I looked very tired, I should get more sleep and relax. He'd been worried about me, he told me, and said I should start accepting invitations to things, so I didn't feel so alone.

— But what about what I saw?

— It's a sign of exhaustion... a trick of the light... déjà-vu... get some rest... stop working so much... stop worrying so much... we all see things that aren't there, especially when we're tired...

A lump came to my throat and I wondered if I was drowning. They looked so concerned for me, but I knew what I had seen. I knew it was real. I knew it *was* Lucy. She had been there, just as she was twenty years before.

So I smiled and said they were probably right. I should start doing things for myself and seeing people again. They smiled back and encouraged me.

One of them said I should come over for Sunday lunch, the kids would love to see me again. That they always ask after me. We could do a roast, and then go for a walk in the park. Maybe we could go for a drink in the pub down the road and have some time together, just the two of us.

I could see it in my imagination. A restful afternoon letting go a little. I *was* tired, I heard my other self say. I could do with some family time. It would help to recharge the batteries.

FOUR

After I got back from that trip, I didn't travel for another month or so. It wasn't my choice. I hadn't wanted to stay at home, to stay still, not after what had happened. I had told no one about the second time I saw Lucy, but the day after I got back, my boss asked me for a quick 'chat' in his office.

I couldn't think what it could be about. The client meeting had gone well, so much so they'd not only re-signed, but also increased their order. What could be the problem?

I walked in and he asked me to close the door. Asked, not demanded. He was talking softly, the way I imagine he does when his son has done something wrong.

He smiled at me, then looked at his computer screen. I sat down and watched him. I knew he was killing time, pretending to check something, so I inspected the yellow and blue stripes on his thick, shiny shirt and his football cufflinks.

— You've been a lot on the road lately, haven't you.

I smiled. I don't know why. I think I was uncomfortable.

— I guess so.

— How are you feeling? You must be very tired.

I cleared my throat and looked at the wastepaper basket in the corner of the room. The discarded carton of a take-away sandwich stuck out of the top. It had been half scrunched up, and then thrown there, I surmised. I knew what he was like, my boss, I knew how he did things. He only ever acted in the moment, never thinking of the one to come. I scoffed at his lackadaisical approach to waste management, and then wondered why I carefully folded my sandwich wrappers, as if they might be used again, before neatly placing them in my bin.

His takeaway coffee cup was still on his desk, even though the dried stains on the outside and the even light cast through the cardboard suggested it had been finished and forgotten a while ago.

I looked up and realised my boss was waiting for an answer.

— I'm okay.

— How do you think the last meeting went? For you, I mean.

— Good. They re-signed and increased their order, so I guess the proof of the pudding is in the fee-ing.

He smiled and nodded. — Absolutely. That's the bottom line, I suppose.

He paused and pretended to check his emails again.

— Chris told me you seemed a little distracted, like you weren't quite there.

— Oh really?

I didn't even remember Chris having been there. Oh yes, of course he was. He led the meetings.

— He told me you said some strange things. Dieter took him to one side at some point and asked if everything was okay with you, whether you might need a rest.

— Dieter asked that?

I stared at the wastepaper basket again.

— I wonder why he didn't say that to my face, I said quietly.

— Because he is worried about you.

I sat up and frowned.

— Surely his behaviour says the opposite. Going behind my back and telling a colleague who might profit from the situation is hardly the action of a friend. He should have talked to me directly. Not that I ever assumed he was a friend. I've always had the impression the only person Dieter worries about is himself.

— I'm sure he didn't mean any harm by it. But he's not the only one to say something. There've been a few comments lately, about how you've been behaving.

— What? What do you mean? Who said what?

— It doesn't matter. It's fine. Why don't you sit down and we can carry on chatting?

I looked around. When had I stood up? My fists were clenched and there was anger in my voice.

— Was I shouting just then?

— A little. Don't worry about it. Just sit down and let's talk.

— I'm sorry, I mumbled and sat down. My mind flashed back to the magnificent parrot and her glass dark eyes shining out from her iridescent black feathers. She titled her head and her feathers rustled. She was staring at me, hard.

I shook my head and tried to focus on my boss and what he was saying.

— ...so just think of it as time to slow down, take stock a little bit. It's not about stepping back or being demoted; it's about you getting a chance to recharge your batteries.

— What, what...? I stammered. — What do you want me to do?

He smiled and placed his hands flat on his desk. Presumably he'd learned in a management training course.

— This is exactly what I'm talking about. You're here, but not here, drifting in and out all the time. I, we, can all see you've been under an awful lot of strain recently, what with the divorce, the move, your father dying. You're all alone there in your apartment and I bet you haven't seen anyone and taken the chance to relax for months, have you?

— Well, I...

— And we've hardly helped, have we? I admit it... He raised his hands like a preacher, palms flat towards me. — We've become overly reliant on you, sending you all over the place to attend meetings, give lectures, glad-hand anyone who comes in arm's length, be the face of the company, and on top of that, manage your own team. And a team that is getting bigger and bigger all the time and, quite frankly, is the engine of what we do here.

I hung my head, unsure what to say or what expression to wear.

— Honestly, it's my fault, all of this. I dropped the ball. I kept pushing more and more on to your plate, expecting you to take it on without considering the impact on you, especially when you've had so much going on yourself. You're our star asset. We can't let you burn out, can we?

I swallowed and stared at him uncomfortably.

— So that's why I think it's time you didn't travel for a while, just for a few weeks. You've got that big conference at the end of the month, so why don't you take time to prepare for it? Really work on that presentation. And focus on the team. They need some time with you, to check in and think through how to take things forward. Maybe you could do some actual work. You know, the job you came here to do in the first place? Before we took you away from it with all that responsibility? You're always moaning about how you never get to do it anymore.

Always moaning? What did he know about me and my thoughts? I stared at his face and his moving lips. What does he know about me? I've never talked to anyone at work about my feelings. Does he know about Lucy? I shuddered and stared at the floor. Could he know about her? Is it possible?

I thought back to who I had told. I was sure it was only those two friends, when we went for a drink. Maybe I said something when I had that quick drink with my team last week. But I only stayed for one. Or I think I did. I got back home pretty late.

But if I wasn't with them, what did I do in between times? I was really hungover the next morning. Maybe I'd stayed in the bar later than I thought. When I finally made it into the office, everyone was looking at me strangely. I tried to be as bright and breezy as I could but they just mumbled and got on with their work.

WHEN I WAS MAKING coffee later that day in the kitchen… well, everyone called it a kitchen, but it was more like a blocked-off corridor with cupboards down one side and a Formica worktop stained with brown rings on the other. Every mug was cracked and chipped, and each chip was stained brown.

There was a mug from a Christmas market in Berlin which I always tried to use. It reminded me of a happy time, maybe one of the only ones, after I had moved to the big city, when I finally got my life together and started to make something of my career. When Lucy and I were working together.

At a dinner party I can barely remember, I made friends with some people over from Berlin for a work placement. We stayed in touch and, one day, I decided to visit them. The first time I went, I stayed in their place, but by the second visit, they'd had a child and so I rented a nearby apartment for a week. It was the first time I'd had some time on my own in Berlin, and I was free.

There is one moment in particular that comes to mind. It isn't much to talk about. I am walking down Danziger Straße towards Eberswalder Straße on my way to meet people in a bar. The bar is just after the U-Bahn station, on the left as you walk along the tramlines. It's the one with the huge windows and lots of doors opening out on to the street.

In the memory, I am walking down Danziger Straße towards the U-Bahn station, calm, happy, light, full of anticipated delight, excited to see my friends. I am taking in everything around me, noticing the people, the bars, the restaurants; the sights, the sounds, the smells; the temperature of the air as I breathe it in; the blue-red sky hanging over the railway bridge. I even notice the texture of the pavement beneath my feet.

I am awake, present, revelling in life and the possibilities it offers.

And then the moment is gone.

— Did you hear what I said?

— I'm sorry, what?

— Did you hear what I just said to you?

He looked irritated and I swallowed nervously. The heat was rising within me.

— I'm sorry. I… I must have drifted away for a second.

— This is exactly what I mean. He sighed — Look, it doesn't matter, we can talk about it another time, when you're feeling more rested.

— But…

— Honestly, it's fine. Take the rest of the day, eh? He checked his computer screen. — Actually, it's Thursday. Take the rest of the week off and I'll see you on Monday.

— But what about…

— It'll all be taken care of. He raised his palms towards me again. — I'll tell the team you're not feeling great or something like that. Go home. Relax. I don't know, maybe watch a film. Go for a walk or whatever it is you like doing when you're not working.

I stared at him.

— You don't do anything when you're not working, do you?

— Well…

— Seriously, you need to start enjoying life. Get a hobby, make some friends. Take up golf. He frowned at me. — You're not the golfing kind, I know. How about painting classes? My wife loves it. He paused and frowned again. — Anyway, go home, forget about this place, and work and presentations. I'll see you on Monday. Okay?

I must have looked doubtful.

— It's okay. Really, it is. It's completely normal for people to burn out from time to time. We all have, especially when we've gone through what you have. And if you didn't burn out after all that, I'd have to wonder what was wrong with you.

He's going to sack me. I was convinced. I glanced at the wastepaper basket and its half-screwed-up sandwich packet.

— Okay, boss. Thanks. See you Monday.

I got up. He got up. I stood and looked at him. He did the same. He thrust his hands in his pockets. I turned and walked out of his office.

That night, I slept for eighteen hours.

FIVE

I WAS HAPPY TO GO TO THE CONFERENCE AT THE END OF THE month. I spent the whole time in the weeks after my 'chat' with the boss wondering what people were thinking about me. Everyone was staring, hanging back from speaking, watching my hands, my mouth, not catching my eye, listening sometimes with a half-smile on their lips.

They were laughing at me.

I knew it.

I tried to get everything right, not to make any slip-ups, to anticipate everything and have all the answers. It was exhausting, but I spent every evening late in the office, reading up on everything again and again, making sure I'd not missed anything.

I thought about Dieter and about Chris. How could they betray me like that? They wanted rid of me, that was clear now. I'd show them; I'd get everything right, every single little thing. Then they'd see. And I'd be funny and smart and engaging, and I wouldn't say anything strange. Not any more.

. . .

I'D WAKE up in the middle of the night in a cold sweat, worried I'd missed something. So whatever the hour, I'd get up, make myself a coffee and go through everything all over again, for every client. I double-checked against every project the company had done for them, even before I got there, looking into all the details.

People noticed. They noticed how much I knew, how aware I was, how I had an answer, the right answer, for every question. They started coming to me to check things, to ask my advice. I stayed longer and longer in the office, got up earlier and earlier.

I worked on my presentation with my boss, and I was enthusiastic. He was pleased; he said I was less hard-headed than before, less irritable. He started to pat me on the shoulder, to smile at me like an equal, not a lost child.

Everything was perfect.

And that's when the problems started.

IT WAS NEVER natural for things to go well, to feel good about myself and my life. I have always felt wrong, out of place, uncomfortable. Like an actor trapped on the stage, sweating under the lights, with the audience out there in the darkness, shifting in their seats. A line is expected, and it is given, but it is not *me* speaking. The line is not mine, and the part is not mine. It has all been a mistake. A terrible mistake.

Unnatural. That's it. I have always felt unnatural. Unnatural inside my skin, as if I am trapped inside the wrong body. Alone inside a body that is not my own, looking out at the world. A world that expects something I am not.

I knew my destiny, my fate. Always to be battling against adversity, overcoming challenges, obstacles, hurdles, negative opinions, and always falling short in some way.

Sometimes I did win. It was a false victory, I knew that.

31

But *they* didn't. They saw me winning and they congratulated me. They saw it had not been easy, that I had overcome adversity. I made sure of that.

And if there was no adversity, no challenge, then I would have to create one and show everyone how well I had done to overcome it. To get up and still perform even if you are incredibly tired, late, hungover, grieving, battling illness, dealing with all that while working yourself into the ground, that is the achievement. Winning when everything is going well is too easy, too predictable.

When I was a child, I was always the outsider. The foreigner with glasses, an inhaler and no friends. My parents didn't help. I was never allowed out on my own or to have anyone over. No birthday parties, no contact with anyone once the school bell rang. I was isolated and alone, unable to interact, always awkward. Never in, always out.

You get used to it. It comes to define you.

I would sit at the edge of the playground and take off my glasses. Everything beyond the end of my nose was blurred so I would pretend the living world didn't exist and disappear into my own universe. I'd forget where I was and made up stories, lives, people, places. I was lost in my imagination. It was the only place I felt safe.

I wouldn't hear the other boys run up behind me. It would be too late by the time I noticed they had taken my bag and trampled on my glasses. They kicked me in the back, and then again and again, rolling me across the hard tarmac. The rough stones dug into my skin, and I would curl up into a ball and let my mind go blank, hoping they wouldn't kick my face, praying my clothes wouldn't be ripped and I wouldn't have to say anything to my mother.

Or something like that.

. . .

I DON'T KNOW if it really happened like that or whether it's a composite of things that occurred and other things I imagined. It's like that sometimes with memories.

We compile small incidents that happened over a period of time into a clear narrative around a single coherent event, when in fact they were spread out over time, occurring in different time and places, and with different people. We do it because it helps us to make sense of things, or explain them to others.

Like now, with you.

When I think about that period of my life, I replay the film *Merry Christmas, Mr Lawrence* in my head. The scenes at school before the Second World War, not when he was in the Japanese prisoner of war camp.

It's not that I wasn't bullied and I'm simply transferring episodes from that film into my life. I *was* bullied. A lot. My glasses *were* trampled on, at least once. I *was* afraid of going home, regardless of whether my clothes were damaged or not. And I *was* kicked, many times. I remember the taste of dust and blood in my mouth more clearly than any other from my childhood. I remember the hard daggers of the stones in the tarmac that dug into my skin. That and the resonating ache of being kicked in the head.

And I *did* take off my glasses to daydream, imagining the blurred reality as kingdoms, laid out across beautiful plains filled with butterflies and wildlife, bathed in eternal sunshine and coursing with shimmering waterways. There was always a magical city just over the horizon. It would help me forget where I was. That was happiness.

I never did make it to the magical city.

. . .

MAYBE I REPLAY those scenes from *Merry Christmas, Mr Lawrence* in my head because it's a safe way of dealing with the events of my childhood, of distancing myself from them and my memories, so I don't have to think about them directly.

DON'T THINK I came up with that explanation myself. Someone suggested it to me. It sounded good, likely even.

But now I'm sitting here wondering whether it's right.

AS I AM WRITING THIS, I can hear sweeping outside in the yard, by the side doors. It must be nine in the morning. I should stop listening to other people work and get on with writing.

I HAVE ALSO BEEN TOLD I deliberately sabotage my life when it's going well so I can return to that childhood state of being always wrong, always unacceptable, always hated, with only myself to rely on.

Loneliness and isolation. That is my comfort zone. I create it when people try to get too close, when they want to love me.

That sounds awful. Can it really be true?

The same person who told me about *Merry Christmas, Mr Lawrence* being a safe place for my childhood memories also told me I am a little paranoid. No, what he said was I have 'paranoid tendencies'. I asked him whether the FBI had told him that after they had been listening to my thoughts using a special brain microphone.

It was a joke. I smiled. He didn't.

. . .

I MUST HAVE BEEN happy to go on the work trip at the end of the month as I researched, maybe for the first time in years, what I would do when I got there. I spent a small fortune on one of the last seats in the stalls to see *Don Giovanni* at the opera house. There was a big-name tenor singing that night, and I'd read the conductor was going places, so they say. I was excited. And nervous.

I get nervous before I travel, which seems ridiculous when you think about how often I took a flight each year. It's the loss of control, I think. Putting your life entirely into someone else's hands. I don't mean in the risk of crashing and dying sense of it. There's nothing we can do about that, so we might as well forget about it.

I am prepared for death.

It's life I find a little more difficult.

No, the risk of death is not the part of flying that bothers me. It's the powerlessness that comes from putting your plans into someone else's hands. Everything you arrange coming to nought because of a late plane, a missed connection, a cancelled train. Sensing everyone clearly thinks you could have made it if only you'd tried harder, if you'd factored in enough contingencies, if you'd planned ahead enough. They always say it could have happened to anyone, but really they mean it happened to you, and to you alone.

EVERYTHING WENT like clockwork on my way to the conference. Everything was on time. But I was still relieved to be in my hotel room, suitcase open on the bed, ready to unpack. I sat next to it, staring at the windows, which covered an entire wall from floor to ceiling. For once, we'd had enough time to go over my presentation a couple of times in its entirety before I got on the plane, and I'd already sent it to the conference organisers for putting into their system for me to use the next day.

All was in order at work and my team was up to date. I had made sure of that. I was exhausted from the effort, but I was relieved I could stop thinking about it. Actually, it was more than relief. I was, for the first time, confident. Confident about my team and confident about my presentation the next day. There was nothing to worry about.

So why the nagging doubt? The little catch in my throat, the tug at my insides from who knows where? I looked up and noticed my better, more worldly self sitting in the corner of the room. He wasn't saying anything but looked rather smug, as if he knew something I didn't.

— What?

I spoke out loud, in the hotel room. It sounded strange, echoing off the windows.

I looked out and noticed the view for the first time. It was impressive. The whole city was spread out before me. It was magnificent, majestic even. The rooftops lay like endless gardens to explore, kingdoms hidden from the world below. I took it all in. That and the beams of sunlight piercing through the heavy clouds. It was rather beautiful.

He was still in his corner. He wasn't looking at me; he was busying himself with something, but he had that smug look on his face.

— What?

— Nothing.

— What do you mean 'nothing'? You always mean something.

— I mean absolutely nothing at all. He smiled at me cryptically. — Go and enjoy your opera, your *Don Giovanni*.

He lingered over the last word, pronouncing it with an exaggerated mocking Italian accent.

— Whatever.

. . .

THE OPERA HOUSE WAS BUSY, and people swarmed around the foyer and the steps and street outside. They were dressed in their finery, their work clothes or their shorts and t-shirts. Some even wore cycling gear. I adjusted my tie when the bell rang and had that delicious surge of anticipation you get when you are about to witness something wonderful performed in public to a full audience. There can be nothing like it.

And there was nothing like it. The tenor was in full force and he toyed with his character, with Leporello, his victims and with us. The orchestra, the singers, the audience and the very fabric of the building were swept along by his arrogant sexual energy. He *was* Don Giovanni, for those two hours or so, and he held us in the palm of his hand. We could all understand how he'd been able to corrupt so many and we all knew we may not have been able to resist in their shoes.

In the interval, I stood at the top of the broad velvet-lined staircase that overlooked the ornate and magnificent foyer and half people-watched, half relived the drama, hotly anticipating what was to come.

The opera restarted, and we—the orchestra, the performers, the audience—edged ever closer to the end, the sense of impending doom rising with every scene, the hand of fate slowly wrapping itself around the throat of the unrepentant sinner.

The dinner party for one commenced. The end could not be far away. As the entrance of the statue approached, I glanced around the audience, wondering if they were as excited as me, if they too waited with bated breath.

I looked along the rows, searching the faces, and then I froze. My heart sank and I could no longer hear the music.

My breath became stuck in my throat. A face I know was there. No, not a face I know, a face I *knew*.

How can *he* be here, of all places? How could he, of all people, be *here*?

I tried to swallow, but my throat was dry. Tears sprang to my eyes, and the sweat formed on my brow. He turned slightly to look at the corner of the stage. The statue arrived and the light emanating from the stage increased. I could see his face a little more clearly now and I was almost sick as I realised there was no doubt. It *was* him. My friend. Just as he had been all those years ago.

— But you died, I cried out.

— Shhhhh, someone hissed somewhere behind me.

My head started to swim. I became aware of eyes staring at me, hundreds of eyes, hundreds of people turning and looking at me, out of the corner of their eyes at first, and then straight at me, boring into me. I wanted to run, to break free of the seat, free of the weight of their eyes, pinning me down, holding me there. I wanted to push past everyone and run up the aisle, out into the foyer and into the cool street beyond.

My soul screamed and I forced myself to look at the stage, just as Don Giovanni took the statue's hand.

— *Your time is up*, the chorus sang.

The stage shook, flames leapt up and Don Giovanni cried out in pain.

— *What strange fear now assails my soul. From where do the flames of horror come?*

The chorus cried out and the whole audience turned and pointed at me.

— *Nothing compares to your guilt*, they sang in unison.

I was fixed, pinned down, unable to move, the sweat pouring down my face, soaking my shirt and my jacket.

I wanted to scream, to run, to be pulled down to hell with

Don Giovanni, where I belong. But I was trapped. I looked across, to my friend from so long ago, before he died, when we were all so happy together, to see his face one more time.

But he was gone, and I didn't know any more if he had ever been there.

SIX

I DID A DRAWING.

They told me to. Actually, they asked me, but you know what I mean. The drawing was of red flames, reaching up to the sky. Red and yellow flames. The sky was burned black and brown. If you stared at the flames for long enough they looked like trees. Red and yellow trees. A forest where the trees are tall enough to get lost in. And if you stared at the drawing for even longer, the trees looked like arms, reaching up to the sky in desperation.

They asked me where I am in relation to the drawing. Where do I figure? I said something about being lost in the flames/trees/arms. They nodded and looked serious.

But it wasn't true. I am not burning in the flames, or lost in the trees, or held by a hundred arms. I am not in the picture. I drew the picture. It's not about me at all.

BACK IN MY HOTEL ROOM, I sat quietly on my bed.

I had been so relieved to get out of the opera house. I almost cried out when we were slowly filing out of our row and up the aisle to the foyer. I nearly pushed past someone at some point, but I realised it was pointless. Where would I go? One place in front in the queue?

So I concentrated on my breathing, inhaling through my nose, imagining the air being sucked down through my chest and spiralling in a circle in my abdomen before slowly exhaling out of my mouth. I learned that technique doing martial arts, when I was a teenager. I wish I had kept that up.

To stop myself from panicking as we inched along the aisles, I inspected the moulded plasterwork on the pillars holding up the lowest rung of boxes. Others talked quietly to a companion, some struck up conversations with the person they were next to in the queue. I wondered how often the paintwork on the pillars was redone, and how much it cost. Then I considered how many other people in the opera house were thinking about that at the same time as me. Five, I estimated.

At least it stopped me thinking about what had just happened. I was grateful I was wearing a dark suit. I hoped the sweat patches did not show too much, although there was little I could do about my matted hair. Best not to dwell on it.

THE COOL AIR. That was a blessed relief, once I managed to get outside. I walked quickly along the streets, sticking to the sides, with my back half turned towards to the buildings, like a stray dog. My evaporating sweat made me cold in the night breeze. It didn't matter.

The receptionist looked at me strangely when I arrived in the hotel. I wondered if she was going to tell me I was no longer welcome and I should pack my bags and leave immediately. I scurried across the wide open space between the entrance and the lifts and anxiously pressed the button several times, dreading the receptionist calling my name out or saying 'Excuse me' with a hint of outrage and disgust, righteous in the knowledge the sinner (me, not her) had been exposed and would receive their (mine, not her) just desserts.

I couldn't look at myself in the lift, despite the relief at not having been accosted and ordered out of the hotel. When the metal cabin drew to a halt and the door was about to open, I caught sight of myself in its mirrored surface. I could see why the receptionist had looked at me strangely. It wasn't out of outrage or disgust. It was pity. I was tired and haggard. My skin was drawn and my eyes looked panicked. I hardly recognised myself.

The lift doors started to close again and I walked out just before they shut.

So there I sat on my bed, looking at my hands, then my feet, then the floor. The carpet was cheap, no matter its pretensions, and there were marks and stains, despite its youth. Maybe I could have a cup of tea. But then I thought of the rattle of the kettle as it boiled and decided against it. I didn't want the silence to be broken.

I rearranged my feet on the carpet and sat back a little. Was that television there before? It must have been. Every room in every hotel has a television. I thought about putting it on, but I didn't want that noise either. No, just me and the faint hum of the air conditioning and the empty minibar fridge.

I sighed. Then laughed. I stood up, shaking my head.

How ridiculous this all is.

I stared out of the window and over the city. The buildings shone in reflected light. The low rise block across the street glowed turquoise from the light of my hotel. The street lights snaked off towards the river, following the narrow alleys and walkways, before turning sharp left behind the old factories and opening out on to the river bank in both directions towards the bridges.

I COULDN'T SEE ALL that, of course. I walked around there last time I was in town and I now imagined it in perfect clarity. It's not such a special place, but I remembered it anyway, like so many of the memories that crowd my mind but don't mean anything. If only they did, then there'd be some value in storing all that information. Maybe I could wipe them selectively and keep only the ones I wanted or those that might serve a purpose.

I wondered how that would work in practice, whether individual memories had a location and could therefore be erased one by one. They are unlikely to exist in individual neurones, as that is not the kind of information they store. And, in any case, that would not really work on a practical basis, as it would leave memories vulnerable to loss due to even the most minor neuronal damage.

And that's not how the brain works. There seems to be a loose, nebulous nature to memories that makes me wonder whether they are stored as a single package, or whether different elements are stored in different locations in the brain, or in different groups of neurones, to be reassembled at the moment of recall.

THINKING ABOUT THAT FOR A MOMENT, let's break an event down and say, for example, that colours are stored in one place, what you hear in another, what people look like in a third place, the layout or topography in a fourth, architectural details in a fifth, the time of day and weather in a sixth (or even separately), taste and smell in a seventh, touch in an eighth and your emotions and thought processes in a ninth.

Maybe that could explain why all sorts of different things can be dredged up by old memories, via seemingly random connections. For example, the time of day your brain compiles one memory may trigger all sorts of other memories that were recorded at the same time of day. And smell is the most powerful trigger, as it resides in the oldest part of the brain and is directly connected to everything, especially emotion.

Perhaps this is why we can rarely remember every last detail about a place or an occasion, only parts of it. Maybe the smell for one memory was never recorded in the first place, or the sound, or the weather, and that's why memories are never complete recollections. Maybe only what we thought of as important, consciously or subconsciously, at the time is recorded.

Take, for example, that moment in the hotel room, thinking about the concept of memory. That was where it first crossed my mind, as I stood there staring out of the window and imagining the street lights snaking down to the river, before heading along the banks in both directions towards the bridges.

It was in that moment I realised that, in my memory of the last time I had been here, I had not recorded the smell of the back streets between my hotel and the river. The memory of that walk was, in fact, almost entirely visual, until much later on, when some sound appears. I remembered it had been cold but not windy, and the sky was clear and the ground wet after rain earlier that day.

And now, as I sit and type, there is the memory of me recalling that memory. I can remember the texture of the surfaces in the hotel room, the lights across the skyline, my dark reflection in the window and the weight of the quiet air. But not the smell of the room.

A POLICE CAR passed by in the street below, lights blaring but no siren. I watched it pass and became aware of myself.

You're tired. More than that. You're exhausted.

I thought back to the Japanese restaurant and it all seemed so absurd. Not just that I thought Lucy was there, but I was so convinced it was her I ran out into the street, looking for her. I hadn't been able to see what had been obvious to everyone else, what they had been trying to tell me for weeks. I needed a rest.

And you've been like this not for weeks, but for years. Ever since the divorce. No, before then, before the separation, years before. Before you realised you'd made a mistake in marrying her. Yet another mistake.

I laughed at the window and saw my dark reflection shudder.

But it all seemed so real. And not just in the Japanese restaurant; in the pizza place, too. That was worse. I thought back to the waitress, her black iridescent feathers and her glass dark eyes staring at me.

Forget about her, it's all over now. You've understood what's happening and you know what to do about it: get some rest.

But what about what happened tonight, in the opera house? What was that?

I paused for a second. It was stress, surely. The fear what happened was going to start again, made manifest. I hadn't acknowledged it beforehand, but I was afraid of coming on the trip, precisely because of the fear *it* would all start again. That I would see her again.

Seek and ye shall find. You created that experience, out of

thin air, out of your own imagination. And you know how susceptible you are to great art. Do you remember how you cried at *Swan Lake*? Or *La Vie en Rose*? Mind you, everyone cried at that. The whole cinema was bawling their eyes out.

I smiled at the memory, and I am smiling now at me smiling at the memory while I'm writing this.

It's a good sign, I told myself in that hotel room, that you can smile about it. You're going to get out of this rut. You're beginning to see the light. And you know what you need? You need to slow down, get yourself in order, get some sleep, and share your life with someone.

But what about Lucy?

And what about *him*? It was him, wasn't it?

My heart sank. I stared at my dark reflection.

My better, more worldly self picked himself up out of the chair by the door, where he had been slumped ever since I came in, and walked over.

— It was just a trick of the light. Both of them had been floating around in your subconscious for a while. You were going through one of those phases when you want to get rid of all the heavy weight of daily life and turn back the clock, to return to a simpler time.

I nodded. He was right.

— Of course I'm right. Now clean your teeth and go to bed. You've got a long day tomorrow and you need some rest.

I looked out of the window again and gazed across the city. It looked different now. Some of the office lights had been switched off, but it wasn't that. I was looking at it differently. I was not looking for signs and making things out of them. I was simply looking, taking it all in.

I felt lighter, content, happy even. I thought about walking along Danziger Straße towards Eberswalde Straße, happily anticipating being with my friends in the bar. That evening in Berlin was cool and the air was light. It had rained earlier on in the day, and the air smelled fresh. I was strolling, not walking. I was smiling at everything and nothing. A train came into the station as I approached the bridge. It rattled noisily and something clicked in my head. I felt pleasure, I felt alive.

— Everything is going to be okay, I said out loud and turned to go to the bathroom.

And then the telephone rang.

SEVEN

I STARED AT THE TELEPHONE. I HADN'T REALLY NOTICED IT WAS there when I unpacked earlier. It was on one of the bedside shelves, presumably the side where most people sleep. I'd put my book on the other side.

They, them.

THEY TOLD me the other day—they've told me before, several times—I focus too much on the small details. *They* say I'm trying to distract myself from thinking about the big stuff, the really important things that are bothering me. It's a kind of delaying tactic, I suppose.

There is no 'suppose' about it, as my father used to say.

What I am trying to say is I wrote that about my book being on the other bedside shelf because I am delaying having to tell you about the telephone conversation. You see, I was immediately nervous, almost shaking with fear down to the pit of my stomach, when I heard the phone ring.

I jumped, of course. I'd been so lost in my own quiet

world, with only the hum of the air conditioning and the empty minibar fridge, that it was a shock to hear the phone.

THERE I AM, doing it again. Delaying talking about the phone call. We know I'm shocked, I've established that, and that I am staring at the phone.

And I did stare at it, rigid, wondering what to do.

I didn't consider picking it up. That was the last thing I wanted to do. No, I wanted to walk straight out of the room, go down in the lift and walk out into the cool night air until I knew it wouldn't ring anymore.

After all, what if it's reception to tell me... what? That I have to leave?

I took a step towards the phone and peered at it, as if it might jump up and bite me. Unknown number. If it was reception, it would surely say so on the little screen.

I stepped back again, feeling foolish. And then it stopped ringing. I sighed and made once again for the bathroom.

The phone rang again. I stopped in the middle of the room and tried to concentrate. Who knew I was there? In the city, maybe a dozen people or more. In that hotel? Three? I thought through them.

Tara, who arranges all travel and accommodation for the company. Maybe her boss knows, too, but probably not. And it would hardly interest her if she did. The conference organisers? Maybe, but it's unlikely they know where I'm staying and even less likely they care. The chair of the session where I will speak tomorrow? Yes, he knows. He emailed me a few times before the trip and casually enquired about where I was staying.

Casually?

The magnificent parrot flashed into my mind and her glass dark eyes shone as they stared into me.

No, it's not the session chair. He has my mobile number and would text me if he wanted to contact me.

So who the hell is it?

— You are clearly not feeling that relaxed and well adjusted, my better, more worldly self said from his chair by the door. — Otherwise you'd just pick up the phone. What can it hurt?

I stared at the chair, and after a few seconds I realised it was empty, and had been ever since I got back from the opera house.

THE PHONE STOPPED RINGING. I sighed and hung my head.

It started ringing again and I went straight over and picked it up. I held the receiver by my ear and waited.

— Thomas.

It was a woman's voice, clear, direct, certain. And it wasn't a question, it was a statement. Even with that one word, I was nervous.

— Yes?

Silence.

— Thomas.

— Yes?

— We should meet.

I froze. A million thoughts crashed through my mind, from the frightening to the ridiculous to the absurd. Who is she? Who on earth can be calling me? I glanced at the bedside clock. It was already after midnight. Meet? When?

This is stupid.

I went to put the phone down.

— Wait.

The receiver was no longer by my ear, but I could hear her voice cutting through the air like a knife. I brought it back up to my ear.

— Can you see me? What is going on?

Silence.

— Who is this?

— I know what you are thinking.

My stomach sank and I could hardly breathe. I swallowed and my throat was thick and tight.

— What do you want from me?

I was stammering. The sweat formed on my brow and gathered under my armpits.

— To meet.

— Why?

— You know why.

— What do you mean? What is this?

Panic rose inside me.

— You know why, she repeated slowly and deliberately. — You know exactly what this is about. You have always known.

My mind flashed back to Lucy. It *was* her, wasn't it?

— How could you possibly know about that?

I could barely get the words out.

— Think about it. Think about all the things that have been happening to you. Think.

I stared at the floor, and then up at the window. I couldn't see the city any more, just my own dark reflection. Another self staring back at me. I could see the phone in my hand, reflected, and I let it fall a little from my ear.

I wanted to put the phone down. I wanted to say I didn't know what she was talking about and end the call there and then. I wanted to put the receiver down, grab my jacket and walk the night off. But most of all, I wanted to clean my teeth, go to bed and sleep, like a normal, well-adjusted adult who is in control of his emotions.

And yet I was frozen in time, waiting for whatever she would say next.

I was a fly, caught in a web.

I lifted the receiver back to my ear to say something, but she spoke before I could gather myself.

— Don't you want answers?

— To what?

— Don't play games with me. You know exactly what I'm talking about.

— But...

— Meet me, tonight. At the last place you were thinking about. In half an hour.

Before I could say anything, the phone clicked off and I put the receiver down. Half an hour? I check the clock. It's half past midnight already.

I have to be up early tomorrow. I have to be at the conference. By eight at the latest. I have to give my talk. Plus, I have to get up early to repack.

I cursed myself for not having left everything in my suitcase, even though I always make a point of unpacking, even for one night, so I feel more at home.

I THOUGHT AGAIN about her voice, about the way she spoke. She was so clear and direct.

I stood there for a moment, staring into the middle distance, and then shook my head and looked out of the window. There was a skyscraper in the far distance. Some of its lights still shone. A plane crossed the sky, somewhere up high. I thought about the conference, and the session chair.

Such a nice man. This kind of thing never happens to him, surely.

I thought of my friends and how absurd I sounded when I tried to tell them about seeing Lucy in the Japanese restaurant. And how kind they had been, trying to help me see I was tired and needed some rest. And I thought about my boss and our conversation, and the time we'd spent together getting my presentation ready.

THEN I REMEMBERED a story someone told me about his great uncle, a lonely academic in Germany who got sucked into an online scam after someone pretending to be a young woman found him on the internet. He went all the way to South America, thinking he was going to find love with a sexy young woman less than a third of his age, who apparently had a thing for old, grey university lecturers.

Instead he was duped into carrying drugs with him in a suitcase he was given to take back to Europe. He spent several months in jail before the sorry tale was unravelled and my interlocutor's family could do something to help him. Idiocy is not a crime, he said, but sometimes it becomes one when it gets mixed up with other people.

No, you can't go and meet her. That's stupid. She must be ripping you off in some way. Maybe she got your name from someone working at the hotel, or maybe she just dialled randomly and guessed. Maybe she's a prostitute or part of a kidnapping ring, not that they'd get much from taking me. Maybe I'm being tempted into a trap. It would be funny, if I wasn't to be the victim.

I thought about her voice. Powerful, measured, sexy even.

You stupid, stupid man. Idiot. Look at you, led around by your stupid fantasies and paranoias, and now, apparently, by your dick.

I looked out over the city and thought about the conference the next day.

Enough thinking, you go to bed and watch a film. You've got your laptop with you. Grab that, get into bed and watch a film. Perfect. Or maybe you can read your book. You've been wanting to do that for ages, and there it is, sitting waiting for you on the bedside shelf. You could even look at the conference programme. No, that's boring. Just clean your teeth, get into bed and then decide what you want to do.

Good idea.

Then I turned, grabbed my jacket and walked out of the door.

EIGHT

I HAVE BEEN THINKING FOR A LONG TIME ABOUT HOW TO WRITE this next part. It's difficult to know where to start or exactly what to say. *They* told me several times simply to write down what I remember, to just recall the events, as I see them.

But that's the problem. I can remember everything that happened that night, down to the second, down to every sensation, even the taste of the air, and every last word, gesture and expression. It's not simply a case of writing it down. If that was all it took, I'd have finished this months ago.

I shied away from writing about it after I recounted the phone call. It was too painful to continue, so I distracted myself, found excuses, told myself I wasn't ready, took ages over things I could have done in minutes, spent hours looking out of the window at the rain falling on to the gardens and the trees beyond.

MANY YEARS AGO, I took a train from Berlin to Leipzig. I think it was for work. I seem to remember being dressed smartly and having a sense of nervous anticipation. But that's just me.

I do wonder sometimes why I force myself to travel so much when I find it so stressful and difficult. Maybe I enjoy the thrill of being outside my comfort zone, forcing myself to do things I don't enjoy to push past my limits and be... what? A better person?

It was the middle of winter. Late January, if I remember, and the snow lay thick on the ground. I squashed myself up against the window and looked out over the fields as they whizzed past, marvelling at the beauty of the snow, as it seemed from our vantage point, with the speed of the train blurring the imperfections into invisibility.

I wanted to walk into it, to experience the heavy silence of the snow, to be alone in the blinding wasteland.

A line of trees, and then the scene opened out to a small field framed by dark forest. Two deer, a doe and its fawn, stood at the far corner of the field, silhouetted against the pure white of the snow. I knew, we all know, that life in deep winter is harsh for wild animals, but from a distance they seemed so still, so calm, so perfect that I would have swapped places with them and given up my life in an instant.

THE PROBLEM with writing about what happened next, when I met her, is to do so requires me to understand and be able to explain what it meant to me at the time. Not only that but also to be able to understand and explain what it means to me now. In some ways, I had no idea then and I have no more idea now.

What happened—what happened to me, how I become embroiled with her and her life—is inexplicable, because I only know it from my perspective. It is incomprehensible, certainly to me, and if it is incomprehensible to me, then it would be to anyone else.

They said that doesn't matter, the act of writing it down will help me understand and explain. I like the sound of that, but it's a little too easy. *They* said the most important thing is I arrive at a point of understanding, whatever form that might take. But my faint ambitions stretch a little further than that.

THE TYPEWRITER BROKE, you know. The one I'd been using to write this. I had started writing this part, happy in my secluded spot, with its ray of sunshine and...

No, actually, I should explain. I wasn't happy, I was nervous. I had been nervous for a while, probably about writing this, but the act of setting myself up in my quiet corner with the typewriter makes me happy. I always come away feeling relaxed and content, even if I start off feeling quite jittery.

But it broke. The typewriter. When I was using it. The return arm. Well, not the return arm itself, but the thin piece of metal that connects it to the carriage snapped, and it could return the carriage no more. I know I had not been writing with any greater force than usual. I know I didn't hit the return arm too hard. *They* said it was just an accident, one of those things, and I shouldn't worry about it. They took it away for repair, promising it would be back in a few days, right as rain.

(I actually don't remember the phrase they used. Maybe they didn't say 'right as rain'. But I like it. My father used it a lot. Before he died, of course.)

I suspected I had done it on purpose—breaking the carriage return arm, I mean. Not consciously, of course, that would be absurd. But subconsciously. That is possible. I wondered if I had been nervous about getting to this part and willed myself to break the typewriter.

I ARRIVED outside the opera house half an hour later. I was surprised to see someone there waiting. I don't know why because she said she would meet me, but it had all seemed so improbable after our conversation on the phone that, when I turned the corner, I was not exactly shocked to see her standing there, but my stomach dropped anyway and I stopped walking.

Much later, it occurred to me she could have been anybody. Turning the corner and seeing someone standing outside the opera house at one in the morning didn't automatically mean it was her, that she was waiting there for me. There could be any number of reasons why someone would wait outside a famous landmark in the centre of town in the middle of the night.

But there I stood, maybe 150 yards away from the entrance of the opera house, staring. Light rain fell, so light initially that I was unaware of it. It was more of a fine mist that seemed to emanate as much from the ground as the sky. The ground shone wet. She was silhouetted by the reflections from the street lamps and the lights around the entrance to the opera house.

She looked out across the square, not up the street towards me, and so was in profile. I couldn't tell much about her from that distance, other than she was small, and had what appeared to be dark curly hair. I stood gazing at her, my mind drifting into all sorts of other spaces, thinking about the sound of her voice on the telephone earlier; my reflection on the window of my hotel room and the city beyond; about the state I had been in since I left the opera. I shuddered at the memory of what I now saw must have been a panic attack.

YET HERE YOU ARE, as you always knew you would be.

My better, more worldly self didn't exactly say that, but his words floated across my mind. No, it wasn't him. He wasn't there. I had been alone ever since the phone had rung. But it was the kind of thing he would say.

And yet there I was. And I didn't know why.

Not really, anyway. I could blandly say I was curious, but that would be meaningless, like saying a lake is wet. Obviously I was curious, but I am curious about all sorts of things and do exactly nothing to satisfy that curiosity.

And yet there I was.

I COULD FEEL the rain now, penetrating my clothes, wetting my face, flattening my hair. It was increasing, the rain. It fell in waves through the light from the street lamps. And I stood, motionless, the idea of moving towards her forgotten. She looked out across the square and I stood in one corner, watching, not even thinking of advancing.

You should turn around and walk away. Whatever this is, whatever she wants from you, it is not going to be good. It is not going to make your life better. You are not going to gain anything. Someone who wants to meet at one in the morning outside the opera house, claiming to know exactly what you are thinking, about what you have been experiencing, and not even having to specify where to meet? That person has nothing to offer you and you should walk away. She is trying to get something from you, to exploit you.

It is too good to be true that someone just turns up and changes your life, that they open a door and you walk

through to an undiscovered land that offers you uncompli-
cated solutions to the problem of being yourself. No, those
people are never the key, the answer to the question.

The answer lies within and is to be found by becoming
happy with yourself and not fighting against who you are.
Those people are a way of avoiding all of that and making
your life immeasurably worse. They are the shortcut to the
well-trodden path of self-destruction. The one that leads you
back to the same old space where you do things you don't
like and you confirm a version of yourself you don't want
to be.

I WISH I'd said all that to myself. It's what I think now, sitting
in front of the repaired typewriter, with sore fingers from
typing too hard and too fast, trying to understand myself and
the decisions I made, not just then, but throughout my life.

If my better, more worldly self had been there, he would
have said something along those lines. But I stood there
alone, trying to think of nothing and not doing what I knew
even then was the right thing to do.

The tiny, malformed, sickly voice of truth, withered and
destroyed inside me, whispered as well as it could that I
should go back to my hotel room.

But I stood there anyway, long enough for the rain to
soak into my clothes and wet my face, but maybe not for that
long in the end. Maybe all that passed in an instant. Like in a
film when the actor's expression changes and you know, you
just *know*, what they are thinking. No explanation required.

But this wasn't a film.

AT SOME POINT, in slow motion, she stopped staring ahead
across the square and turned towards me. Although she was

more than 400 yards away and I could only see her silhou-etted by the street lamps and the lights around the entrance to the opera house, my heart stopped. I could tell she was staring at me.

At me.

My mouth ran dry and I thought I would start crying, as if all the emotion of the last few weeks and months would pour out of me in a flood.

And then, one in front of the other, slowly, deliberately, as if being controlled by an outside force, my feet walked towards her, dragging me like a reluctant child. She became clearer; as I approached, I could see her dark curly hair and her round dark eyes shining. I could not look away, and I wished and wished and wished I had turned around and left.

But the tiny, withered voice of truth whispered to me I had always wanted this. And as I saw her up close, and she shifted her position, swaying on her hips to look straight at me, so seriously and so coldly, I knew it was too late.

I had already fallen.

NINE

It was only after I had finished writing that, maybe several days later, I realised 'fallen' could be taken in two ways. I meant fallen in the sense of down the rabbit hole, or fallen from grace, to have become subsumed by something. However, I think most people, maybe even me if I didn't know what had happened, would think 'fallen in love'.

I have thought about that many times. Did I fall for her? Then or ever? I don't think so. But to be honest, I don't really know. If the feeling that accompanied knowing her is love, then I loved her. But it was unlike any feeling I had ever had before, certainly unlike any 'love' I had experienced.

There was no tenderness on my part, and certainly not on hers. We never discussed our hopes and dreams. There wasn't any affection. I don't think I even liked her. Those sorts of emotions were not part of the equation. They were by-the-by.

No, more than that. It was as if affection had no relevance to how we felt about each other. I was simply drawn to her. (You can choose your own cliché to further colour the sentence, if you like. I thought of 'like a moth to a flame' but maybe you can think of something better, more original.)

IN REALITY, I found her irritating, arrogant, self-centred, pushy, incredibly self-confident and self-assured, dismissive of anyone else's feelings, and she was obviously only interested in someone in terms of what they could do for her. In fact, I have the impression she only ever interacted with, responded to, or solicited the company or opinions of someone if she thought it would directly benefit her and forward her plans.

If she had been anyone else, I would never have spoken to her again. I would certainly never have entertained the idea that we would... but we were never friends. And I never loved her. I didn't even liked her.

So, why? Why did I go to meet her outside the opera house at one in the morning? Why did I go although my better instincts told me not to? Why did I not turn away and walk back to my hotel when I hesitated at the corner of the square? Why did I go to her when she turned towards me? Why did I not walk away as soon as she looked at me up close, staring deep into me, and I knew this was my last chance to leave?

It would be easy to say I don't know. That's what we often say if we find something we have done inexplicable when we consider it in the cool light of day, with the benefit of hindsight. But the truth, the quiet secret, is we make decisions in the heat of the moment with another part of our brain, another version of ourselves; a version we may not like. One we don't want to admit to; one we know does not stand up to scrutiny, certainly not when discussed out loud.

But I know why, really, I didn't walk away. Why I kept on going towards her. I was infatuated, utterly infatuated. Not with her, never. But with the idea of surrendering myself to someone or something, of subsuming myself and disappearing, from myself as much as from the world at large. Not having to carry the luggage of me around with me all the time.

She gave me that.

— WHAT DO YOU WANT?

She smiled, slightly, and with only her mouth.

— What do you want? I repeated.

She looked out across the square, and I followed her gaze. There was nothing and no one, just the light reflecting off the wet pavement. She turned back to me and I saw her eyes were dark pools. Her face softened.

— I don't want anything, Thomas. It's you who came here. It's you who wants something.

I stared at her, confused.

— Why did you come? she asked softly.

— Because you told me to.

— Bullshit. She screwed up her face in a snarl. — You don't do anything just because someone tells you to. You chose to come. Why?

A thousand thoughts raced across my mind. I tried to pull myself together.

— Curiosity?

— Stop playing games.

— I'm not playing games. I don't know what you mean. And how did you know where I was thinking about when we were talking on the phone? How did you know where to meet?

She smiled, the same slight smile. Her eyes stared straight at me, unflinching, hard now.

— I saw you tonight, at the opera. I saw what happened to

you. When did it start?

I stared back at her and swallowed. I wanted to talk, to open up, to ask the question that had been on my lips for months now, but I couldn't bring myself to.

This must be a trick. She can't know anything about that.

— Who are you?

— One thing at a time. When did it start?

— I don't know what you're talking about.

I was nervous now. I wanted to run, to escape her, but I didn't know if I could. If she'd found me here, maybe she would be waiting for me in the next place. Maybe she would turn up and phone me again, and again.

— Were you there?

— Where, Thomas? Now she was calm, quiet, reassuring. I hesitated and tried to regard her objectively.

— How do you know my name?

— Why does it bother you so much?

— I don't know who you are. I don't know how you found me.

— All in good time. Where was I?

— Were you there the first time it happened?

— When what happened?

How could I explain it? How could I express in words? The last time I had tried, I'd felt stupid and humiliated. I went to speak, but the words got stuck in my throat. I became aware of the rain again. My clothes were wet and cold. I shuddered and looked away.

— Are you cold?

I gazed at her. Her face was warm, as if a light had been switched on in her soul.

— No, I'm okay.

— Why don't you tell me what happened, Thomas?

— It sounds stupid.

— Do you mean you're scared to tell me?

I swallowed and stared at her. I willed her to be genuine, to want to help me.

— It's okay, she continued. — There is a truth you have seen, but don't understand, which makes you afraid even to think about it. But you know it wasn't just you being crazy, don't you? You know it really happened. Don't you?

I nodded.

— People have doubted you, haven't they, Thomas. They've made you feel stupid.

I nodded again.

— What did they say? That you were tired? That you must have been seeing things? That you need to get some rest and then it will all go away? But it didn't go away, did it. It didn't stop. It happened again. Didn't it.

I cleared my throat, now thick with emotion.

— Yes, I said quietly.

— And what did you do when it happened again? You tried to forget about it, to pretend it wasn't real, that your eyes were deceiving you. But they weren't.

My mind flashed back to the Japanese restaurant and Lucy smiling and laughing, and my stomach sinking as I knew, for a fact, it was her. I thought about the empty table in the pizza place. She had been there. I knew it. How could the waitress say the table had been empty? How? How?

And I saw the magnificent parrot. She stood right in front of me, her dark iridescent feathers shining a rainbow of blackness, black feathers around her glass dark eyes staring back at me.

— You are not alone, Thomas.

I stared at her, hardly able to breathe as the air caught in my throat, the tears at the edges of my eyes, already wet with the fine rain that fell all around.

— Tell me about tonight.

— It happened again.

— Yes?

— I saw someone...

— Who was it?

— Someone who died, years ago.

— How long has this been happening, Thomas?

I stared at her, afraid and desperate.

— I don't know. Months?

— I saw you tonight, Thomas. I saw what you went through.

— Why is this happening to me?

— It's not just you. You are not alone.

— I don't know what to do.

The tears rolled down my face.

— You don't have to do anything. You are not alone anymore. You are safe now. Why don't you ask me the question? The one you've wanted to ask for all these months.

I stared at her and hesitated. I didn't know if I could go through with it. But she looked at me so calmly, so clearly.

— Why do I keep seeing people from my past, as if they were here now, as real as you and me, just as they were when we knew each other?

TEN

I DREAMT A LOT THAT NIGHT, AFTER I MET HER IN THE SQUARE.
I dreamt I was being chased, sometimes I was chasing. I
never knew my pursuers and I never knew who I was pursu-
ing. I was lost, always. Unknowing of where I was going and
where I had come from.

I've had the same dream, or parts of it, many times. It takes
different forms. Sometimes I am in a landscape, chasing or being
chased down corridors, up stairs, through buildings I recognise,
some I don't. There are people I know, people from the news or
from films I have seen. Once, I managed to construct an entire
harbour in my imagination from places I had known.

IN ONE VERSION of the dream, I start running, running,
running in a village where I lived as a child, all grey stone
and cold façades, streets going nowhere and hills rolling over
the horizon. I run downhill, through a part of a mediaeval
town and into a city built from all the places I have ever
known. A street from my university town, a building from

my adolescence, the train station near where I lived when I first moved to the city.

The river is gone; in its place a vast harbour, elements of a Normandy village mixed up with constructions in metal and glass and, in the middle, a giant Ferris wheel that is also a tower and a rocket pointing up into the sky.

On and on I run, through endless buildings, up and down stairs with locked doors on every floor, along corridors where there is no one and no exit, then down to the harbour, always running just ahead of unknown pursuers.

I reach a flight of stairs, and begin to climb. I climb and climb and climb, now far above the harbour and the city beyond, far into the sky. Then the Ferris wheel/tower/rocket floats off into the ocean, away from everything I have ever known, away from any chance of escape. And I know my pursuers are not far behind.

THAT NIGHT, after I met her in the square, the dream started in the hotel, somewhere on the back stairs. I must have made that part up or used a previous memory because I only ever took the lift.

Down the stairs I run, through a corridor and up another flight of stairs that lead to a rain-soaked street at night, or at least in darkness.

WHEN I FIRST RECOUNTED THAT dream, in its original form, I said that part about the street being 'at least in darkness'. *They* asked me what I meant, and I said it is only by convention that darkness means night-time. If it became dark suddenly at two in the afternoon, we wouldn't say it was night-time, would we? In my dreams, it is often dark, but I know it is not night-time. It is the middle of the day, but it is dark.

I received no response to that statement, neither verbally nor facially. Just a blank stare that could have meant a million things, but probably meant nothing.

Undeterred, I continued that a bat would say our night-time is its daytime, and our day its night. That is because what we mean when we say daytime is not necessarily that the ambient light is over a certain luminescence that allows us to carry on our activities without additional illumination, but that it is the portion of the solar cycle when we are typically awake and going about our business. On the other hand, night-time, though it may be symbolised by a darkening veil over the world, really refers to that part of the day when we do not work and take our daily rest.

My interlocutor sat up at that point, cleared his throat, approximated an expression that suggested something akin to slight constipation and asked if, in my dream, I was a bat. I assumed he was being deliberately obtuse and ignored the question.

Then I uttered something outside the range of human hearing and flew away.

OUT IN THE RAIN-SOAKED, darkened streets, I run, and run, and run, unsure of where I am going or what I am looking for. Turning a corner, I am surprised to find myself on the square where I met her, the woman, but on the other side.

I look for myself standing on the corner but I am not there. I wonder if I have arrived before myself, and I watch her waiting, apparently looking in my direction but not seeing me. I try to see the time on the clock in the middle of the square, but the face is blank.

. . .

THIS IS the point when all those dreams converge. No matter how they start, whether I eventually run down to the harbour or not, I find myself on the square, staring at the clock with the blank face.

Occasionally, when I realise I have reached this point in the dream, I have a sense of awful sense of dread, knowing what has happened, what is about to happen, again and again, time after time, inevitable and constant.

If I am sufficiently conscious, I try to steer myself away from the square and into another dream, where I might feel safe and calm.

It never works.

I AM NOT STANDING in the corner of the square and I don't know what time it is. But she is standing there, waiting for a version of me. Perhaps the reason she was so oblique yet all-knowing when I spoke to her that night, after the terrifying episode in the opera house, is I had already explained it to her before I arrived.

Perhaps I had already been to the square and poured my heart out and, when I hesitated for so long in the corner of the square before approaching her, I did not realise this was the second time I had spoken to her.

IN THE DREAM, I walk towards her. Halfway across the square, I hesitate. She is looking in my direction, but she seems not to see me. She is looking through me. And yet when I do finally arrive in front of her, she regards me as if she already knew what I was going to say.

After we talk for a moment, although I never know what I say or how she responds, I say:

— Why do I keep seeing people from my past, as if they

71

were here now, as real as you and me, just as they were when we knew each other?

At this point in every version of the dream, she smiles and tells me I need to pay attention because she is going to tell me something that will sound so bizarre and outlandish I will find it difficult to believe. However, I must hear her out, as she wants me to know the truth I am so desperately seeking.

She asks me to describe exactly what happened the first time, and so I tell her, in great detail, about everything that occurred when I was in the queue for the Japanese restaurant and I saw Lucy. When I get to the part about Lucy looking at me and me realising it wasn't just someone who looks like her, but it *was* her from twenty years before, she nods her head solemnly. I finish recounting my story and she tells me that it's not the first time she has heard a story like that and they are, in fact, becoming increasingly common.

It is undeniable, she says, there is a pattern, and she and people like me have been searching for several years now for answers. She explains it is people who travel a lot, like me, who notice it most often, but people are seeing it even in their everyday lives.

I demand to know what she means, and she asks me if I am ready to accept a truth that will seem impossible.

I hesitate, but then I say I am.

She stares into me and tells me the human race is being replaced, one by one, by androids. She says there are dark and dangerous forces out there that want to take over the world, person by person, town by town, city by city, country by country, continent by continent, until they have control of every government and power in the world.

To do that, they want to get rid of all humans. They don't want a war, and they certainly don't want any destruction and wanton bloodshed. They want the world intact, perfect and purified of the stain of humanity. So they've come up with an ingenious plan to replace the human race with exact replicas, filling up the 'background' of our lives, bit by bit, so we don't notice there are fewer and fewer of us. Until there are so few of us it will be too late.

Their reasoning, she says, is humans don't interact with more than ten per cent of the people around them, sometimes even less than five per cent, so until there are so many androids that it is too late, there is very little danger of anyone stumbling across the truth. Of course, in some circles, that is more difficult than in others, but it is all about achieving a critical mass of androids until they are ready to take over.

She says every time we eat in a restaurant, go shopping, watch a film in the cinema, take a walk in the park or have a drink in a bar, already somewhere between sixty and eighty per cent of the people that surround us are not real. They are androids, filling up the spaces and our margins of our consciousness.

I look around me, afraid of what I might see.

— Make no mistake, she says, this is a takeover, a revolution, and the entire human race is being wiped out one by one.

Horrified, I ask about the dark forces behind it all, and she tells me there was an explosion, a nuclear explosion, in the middle of the desert sometime in the twentieth century. The terrible energy it unleashed combined with the remnants of a now-lost ancient civilisation to create a cloud of pure evil.

The cloud painted the day sky dark and seeped into the ground, turning it dark. All the plants turned dark and the animals too, and the darkness spread until it reached a secret military base where experiments into android technology were taking place. There, the darkness seeped into the scientists and the military commanders and they saw in an instant where the darkness could take them.

— And now, she says, her eyes burning with dark flames, — they have become so powerful they have even replaced the President of the United States of America with an android.

I step back, stunned, my head swimming.

— But what has this got to do with seeing my friend? I ask, afraid to know the answer.

She tells me it is simple. The way the forces create androids with the appearance, mannerisms, habits and body language of people so realistic they can fool us completely is they scan real people's brains, mining their memories.

She explains that every time we go to hospital or visit an airport or walk through a shopping centre, there are scanners everywhere. The recent terrorist attacks were really a cover to install a highly sophisticated scanning system in every street across the heart of the city. This is the first time they have tried something so daring and bold, but it underlines how confident they are in their plans.

— They must be close to achieving their goal, she says, staring straight into my soul.

SHE TELLS me their objective is to scan our brains while they check us for explosives or take an X-ray of our chest or when we enter into a shopping mall. They pick up thousands of memories we have of a person or several people, ideally from our long-forgotten past, and use them to make android copies that are so lifelike and perfectly human it is impossible to tell them apart from the real thing.

Normally they create androids that will be deployed in different countries or even different continents from where the memories were extracted, to reduce the chance we will come across a human copy made up from our memories.

But as I travel so much, to so many different countries and places, it was inevitable I would come across someone from my past life at some point. The fact it has happened twice in quick succession, with a double copy of the same memory, is a one in several million chance, she adds, but it can happen.

This, of course, means my life is in danger, because if they realise, the next time my brain is scanned at the airport or train station, I am in the vicinity of several android copies derived from my memories, they will seek me out and kill me.

I ask her how she knows so much about this. I consider asking about the magnificent parrot, as she is before my eyes once more, her glass dark eyes shining from within her black iridescent feathers. But I am becoming dizzy and struggling to concentrate on what she is saying. The blood is pounding in my head and I am nauseous.

— Like I said, we have been studying this for a while.

— How did you know about me?

— One of your friends told us. He was worried about you. He is one of us, but he didn't want to reveal that to you until he'd had a chance to inform me.

I think back to the drink in the bar with my two friends and the invitation to Sunday lunch.

Maybe he would have told me all about this then. Maybe I could have known about this before and things would be different. If only I had gone to meet them.

— I'VE BEEN WATCHING YOU, waiting for the right moment to make contact, she says. — When I saw you in the opera house this evening, I knew, finally, it was the right time.

I stare at her, so intently all I can remember now of that moment, as I sit here and type, is her dark eyes, like infinite pools, and the curls of her dark hair hanging down over her porcelain face.

— What do you want from me?

— For you to join us, to join our revolution. To fight the dark forces trying to take over the world and save humanity.

— Why me?

— Why you? We need you, Thomas.

I stare at her, and then look around, aware of the square, the soft rain, the reflected light and the cold penetrating me. I swallow. I look back at her and see she is waiting for an answer. Out of the corner of my eye, I see myself hesitating at the edge of the square, unsure whether to meet her.

Then I turn around and walk away. I keep on walking, even though she calls after me and I desperately want to turn back.

AT THIS POINT in the dream on that night in the hotel, I woke up. All those things she said—can she actually have meant them, or had I made the whole thing up? Did I really go to the square at all, let alone twice.

I looked across my hotel bedroom and saw my wet clothes drying, and my heart sank.

Darkness lay outside the hotel window.

I knew it was still night, but I was already afraid of the day to come.

ELEVEN

WHEN I WOKE THE NEXT MORNING, THE SENSE OF IMPENDING dread was almost overwhelming, although dread of what I did not know. It was a kind of anxiety that bordered on fear. Fear of thinking about what had happened the night before. And of her.

What if it's all true and there *is* a dark force out there replacing every person on earth, one by one, with androids drawn from our memories? But what if none of it's not true? What would *that* mean? And how did she find me? I walked away from her, but if she found me once, surely she will find me again.

I DON'T REMEMBER what I was doing when that occurred to me. Maybe I was cleaning my teeth, or zipping up my suit-case. Perhaps I was checking around the room one more time before I left. All of those sound plausible. I surely did all of those things. But let's say I spun around, after I had that thought, and stared at the corner of the room with the chair.

It's a simple visual image, easy to construct in your mind. Perhaps that's why I constructed it.

So I spun around and hoped, willed, to see my better, more worldly self sitting there—perhaps lounging, as that's more his style—to offer if not comfort, then some advice, delivered in his traditional sarcastic manner. But he was not there. A part of me was not there. I had been split into fragments, and at least one part of me had disappeared.

I turned to the window, which was filled with the light of the day.

There was no reflection now.

SOME ASPECTS of the morning after I left my room I don't remember at all; others are so clear, it is as if they are burned into my mind.

In the hotel, downstairs, in the area beside the reception desk, where the light was stronger and I could banish for a while the shadows that seeped into my mind, I took my breakfast. I wanted to say 'as usual', but what can be usual about having breakfast in a hotel? Unless you live the kind of, if not nomadic then peripatetic, lifestyle I had fallen into.

Had.

Fallen.

AT BREAKFAST, then. Eggs, already boiled, waiting under a lamp that kept them at an even temperature, with a smiley face drawn on each of their shells; a buffet of local cheeses and a range of 'salad items'. I suppose I should call them that in lieu of a better name. And a coffee machine, baskets of bread and rolls. You get the idea.

· · ·

WHEN I WAS A YOUNG MAN, I moved from what was technically my home town to another town, although neither was ever really home. The pretext was to go to university, but actually it was merely the most advantageous and prestigious means of escape I could identify.

I was young and naïve. Wet behind the ears, my father would say. But I'd seen enough that I thought I could bluff my way through life and hide my naïvety, which in itself is a sure sign of naïvety.

I made friends, or I assumed they were at the time. Let's say, with the benefit of hindsight, they were people I hung about with, and they hung about with me. Many years later, I realised none of us knew what we were doing, and had no idea whether we were friends or not. We were so afraid of our big new lives that we had no capacity to judge. At the time, I thought I was the only one who felt that way. I guess they were better at bluffing than me.

The first week after we arrived at university, we took our bikes out and rode into the countryside, having been assured a village lay in that direction. It was a warm autumnal day, but that is all I remember in any great detail. I don't know how many of us there were, or where we went. What I do remember is we stopped to buy lunch. I had not thought about eating lunch or preparing for it in any way, and was surprised at myself for having not considered food as a necessary part of the journey.

Inside the café, I waited my turn, nervous at having to speak out loud to a third party in front of these people who I had arbitrarily decided were my friends just because they were the first people I'd met who hadn't rejected me. The woman behind the counter wore a pinafore over her blouse. She had a white hat on her head to cover her hair. She reminded me a little of the women who worked in my old school kitchens.

It was my turn. I was the last to order. All eyes were on me, fixed, blank, judging. I pointed to the glass-fronted counter and asked for a cheese cob. She did not know what I was talking about, and I had to think of a word we both knew. I came from a place fewer than 70 miles away, and yet there were limitations in our ability to converse in the same language. I didn't dare turn to look at those people I called friends. Some of them were sniggering.

AT BREAKFAST IN THE HOTEL, I stood in front of the cheese and salad buffet, hesitating, my back to the tables ranged behind me, thinking about all the eyes on me, fixed, blank, judging. I was unsure of myself and of what I wanted. I didn't want my usual breakfast. I was not my usual self.

— Good morning. How are you today?

I turned, jolted out of my thoughts, and stared. A young woman who worked on the hotel reception was standing next to me, smiling. I had noticed her before. She was a hesitant person, but obviously kind, and always said hello when I passed, with a slight dip of the head and a timid smile.

Now, listening to her speak, I noted she was Eastern European, probably Ukrainian. Her long, slim fingers wore no jewellery and there were no traces of where rings might have been. She wore stud earrings, no necklace and no make-up. Blonde hair tied back. A smile playing around her sparkling blue eyes. She sparkled.

She was not speaking anymore. She was waiting and smiling.

— Oh, hello. You surprised me. I'm not awake yet. I haven't had my coffee.

I smiled and gestured awkwardly at the machine. Why am I sweating and shaking? Can she see it?

— Are you enjoying your stay? It is your second time

here, isn't it? You were here in June. I remember. It rained a lot and you borrowed one of our umbrellas.

— Yes, I laughed. — You've got a good memory. I remember you, of course, but you must see so many guests.

She smiled and stepped forward to straighten out a plate of cucumber slices. She titled her head slightly and feathers appeared around her neck, like an Elizabethan ruff. As she turned towards me, they fanned out around her hair and over her body. Beautiful iridescent white feathers. She smiled again.

— I don't remember all our guests. They are not all so… memorable.

She stretched out a shimmering white wing towards another plate, this one half full of tomato slices, and I worried she might knock it off with her wingtips. The blood ran cold in my veins and I became dizzy. There was a sort of darkness creeping in from the edge of the room. I was safe here, standing beside her.

She regarded me curiously, with a hint of concern in her sparkling blue eyes.

— It's nice to be remembered, I said eventually.

She shook her head and the feathers reached her face, up around her eyes, now glass bright and shining, catching the colours of the lamps and the boiled eggs. I glanced around the room and saw everyone was staring at us, me and the magnificent dove.

They could all be androids.

Fear gripped my throat and held it tight. I looked back at the magnificent dove and she lifted her head, her iridescent white feathers shaking, to gaze at me.

— I think I'm going to be late for my conference, I heard myself say from somewhere underwater. — I had better go.

— Okay then. The magnificent dove fixed me with her

glass bright eyes, and settled her wings in a rustle of feathers.
— Have a lovely day. I hope to see you later.

I mumbled something and stumbled out of the breakfast room. An overweight, angry man, tight in his alcohol-red skin, stared at me with hatred as I passed. I was overcome with nausea and thought I would vomit.

OUT ON THE STREET, the cool air calmed me, but I could sense the panic building inside me. I was walking okay, I could feel my hands and my feet. I had my bag. I knew I was walking in the right direction for the conference centre. But my clothes no longer fitted. My feet were uncomfortable in my socks and shoes. My skin belonged to someone else. The air was artificial, unnatural in my lungs.

I tried to smile at a woman pushing a buggy as she passed, but it must not have come out right as she looked scared.

Maybe she's an android.

Another angry man, this time on the other side of the road.

Maybe he's an android.

I crossed a side road and almost walked out in front of a taxi as it turned from the main street. He, the taxi driver, was dressed in a pale beige shirt under a bright blue jumper, his greying black hair swept to one side with gel, a pair of glasses on a cord resting on his chest. His face, freshly shaven but not moisturised. His hands gripping the steering wheel with swollen joints and rough skin. They weren't drivers' hands.

He, the taxi driver, looked at me, ready to be angry at me for being so stupid as to walk out in front of him, but his face dropped to empty curiosity when he saw mine.

Maybe he's an android.

A crow jumped across the road, heading I don't know where.

Surely not. It's only the humans they're after.

A café that could have sold me coffee, but couldn't because it was shut. I also had no money and would have needed to pay by card.

I was hungry now, and I needed coffee.

I tried to remember if there had been any coffee places near the conference centre the last time I came here. But I couldn't remember. Not then and not now.

I couldn't remember anything, I could only see what was in front of me. Lines and lines of red bricks one on top of the other, rising up into walls. There must have been other walls because there was a roof. I suppose they were buildings but I was no longer sure. Maybe they are hiding giant scanners, mining my brain for other people to copy, to turn into androids.

A man in a suit, with no face.

Strange. Can he be an android?

And a woman, also with no face.

I tried to think of Danziger Straße and that perfect evening as I walk to meet my friends, but the roads lead nowhere. Eberswalder Straße and the U-Bahn are no longer there. Just a blank wall at the end of the road. Where are my friends? The street is silent and nothing moves, every person, every car, every bird held in freeze frame.

I SHOWED my badge to the security guard on the door of the conference centre, but he didn't look at it. He was distracted by one of his colleagues having a heated discussion with a third. I just wrote 'colleague', but I meant delegate. He was a delegate, the colleague was a man, and they both had blank faces. But you knew that already, didn't you?

Maybe they're androids.

I walked into the conference hall. Light was streaming

down from above, from the skylights that line the roof. It reflected off the shiny floor and bounced everywhere. The light dazzled and disorientated me.

Now, when I think back to that moment, I don't remember which city it was in, what country even. I don't remember which conference it was, what it was about and how I got there.

I do remember walking down the steps into the main open space, which the organisers called, and is often called, the plaza. It's a bit pretentious, but the idea is to give the sense of a little town that has all been created for us delegates. It is supposed to put us at ease.

In the plaza, someone was making coffee on one of the stands. I approached, aware of every muscle in my body contracting and relaxing with each step. The reflected light cut into my eyes like shards of glass. Everywhere I looked, there were people, milling about, talking, consulting the conference programme, making phone calls or people watching. Some people were in groups or pairs, others were alone. But none of them, not one of them, had a face.

How many of them are andr...?

Never mind, I can't think about that now.

At the conference stand where a person was making coffee, I stood waiting, afraid to look at anyone, afraid of their faceless faces. I stared at the floor. It was raised here and covered with carpet squares in mottled red. Between the carpet squares were dark lines, pointing everywhere.

— Next.

I looked up, smiling. I know I was smiling because I remember my muscles contracting and my mouth being pulled up at the edges into what we have all agreed is the most appropriate shape to convey pleasantness, whether or not it is genuine. But I don't know what it looked like to anyone else, or how successful I had been in approximating this well-known expression; I don't know the reaction it provoked, because the barista had no face.

Before I continue, I wonder, is that a received idea? That all the faces were blank, that there *were no faces*? It can't have been true, can it, that no one in the plaza had a face that day?

Think about it practically. Take the barista as an example: how could someone without a face get a job serving coffee at an exhibition stand in a conference? It's not possible, is it? How would the interview proceed?

And let's not forget that he, for it was a he, spoke. He said, 'Next'. And how would such a sound have been created if he didn't have a mouth? From where could that solitary, yet so meaningful, word have emanated?

Don't say the obvious answer. It's beneath you. This is a philosophical discussion, after all.

No, by logical deduction, and remembering everyone has, in reality, a face, I have a number of possible explanations. My mind may have not committed the faces to memory, or blanked them out at the time, before the memory was created. Or is it during my current recall of that moment, as I type, that their faces are obliterated? Whatever the reason, there are no faces in any of the versions of this event, as I recall them.

To return to my previous question as to whether the concept of blank faces is a received idea: Have I seen imagery of faceless people in the past? Undoubtedly. Have I attached some meaning to that experience? I would have thought so.

Blank faces would suggest, what? Isolation? Detachment? Separation from those around us, and even from reality? Did I experience those types of sensations at the conference? Yes.

So perhaps I have used the concept they had no faces as a shorthand way of explaining that without having to write any of this.

A VOICE BELONGING to me asked for a double espresso and the barista said something that sounded like broken glass being ground into the dirt.

How could he speak? He had no face.

The light refracted round and round the room as it fell through the skylight like a waterfall and smashed into a million tiny drops on the shiny floor, scattering and bouncing off every surface. It was absorbed again and again until all that was left was shadows.

A big clock hung over everything. Its arms moved slowly, but inexorably. I took the coffee, and I saw I was late to give my lecture. I thanked the faceless man and hurried away to a space constructed out of room dividers that looked like a sheep pen, but had been given a number, had seats placed inside, as well as a lectern and a screen. We were supposed to think of it as a lecture theatre.

I hurried and tried to drink my coffee, and remember who I was.

As I GOT CLOSER to the lecture theatre, I became increasingly nervous. The light reflecting from all directions blinded me as I passed. I was nauseous and wondered if I could make it all the way across the plaza to lecture theatre number 31. Or 13.

It was just in front of me now. I could see people sitting waiting in the audience. I wanted to run; I didn't know where or why. I wasn't afraid of giving the lecture. Or was I? I don't know. But that's not what I was thinking about at the time. The lecture theatre seemed like a giant ball of energy that repelled me as I got closer. I wanted to vomit, to run, but my legs carried on walking.

I didn't vomit and I didn't run. How? Under what volition?

As I reached the threshold, or the gap in the room dividers that constituted the entrance, I forgot about the fear. And the nervousness. And the nausea. I had entered the ball of energy.

It was calm in there. There was less noise than in the plaza, and less light. I looked around, initially disorientated. Someone approached me before I'd had a chance to collect everything together in my mind, and I must have looked surprised. He stepped back and frowned at me, then smiled.

It was the session chair. I saw that now. Thankfully he had a face, otherwise I would not have recognised him. A complete face. He spoke. He must have done. I saw his mouth move. But I didn't register what he said.

I spoke in response. I must have done. He had an expression that said: I'm listening.

I remembered the magnificent dove and her glass white eyes. I was warm inside when I thought of her. Reaching out my hand, I took her wing, and I was safe. The man, the session chair, must have said something reassuring, as I said 'Thank you' and 'You're welcome'. (I heard, somewhere behind me, the faint shaking of white feathers.)

Then I turned to the audience, or rather the rows and rows of chairs ranged in front of me, the space down the middle forming an aisle, representing an audience as soon as someone sits down in one of the chairs.

And sat they had, the audience, in the chairs. A sprinkling? A smattering? You pick the word. Let's say there were around one hundred and twenty chairs and approximately twenty people sitting in them. Twenty people in twenty chairs would have been a lot. Twenty in one hundred and twenty chairs is just enough to feel like we are not all wasting our time.

ONCE, many years ago, I saw a lecture at a conference given by an expert in psychiatry. It was in a room improbably far from the main part of the conference and was on a topic that, given the conference in question, one might kindly have called 'specialist'. It took fifteen minutes to get there from the loose collection of stands and exhibition spaces that had been called the plaza, and I had hoped the audience would fill up a little more before the expert started speaking as there were only four of us in a room that could hold five hundred at least.

It did not fill up. Four we remained, including the session chair, who was a model of attentive listening. Of course, the presenter had to give her lecture. She had no choice. She was a professional. So she gamely continued as if the room was full of like-minded enthusiasts. It ended up being one of the best things I saw that day.

I wondered at the time whether being an expert in psychiatry might help to shield her from the feelings of humiliation and inadequacy us mere mortals would surely experience at drawing such a small audience. But when I asked her a question at the end, when we were face-to-face and after the session chair had congratulated her on her talk, I saw her training had not shielded her.

She was stressed and exhausted by the effort she had made to deliver a confident and compelling lecture and not give in to her worst thoughts. And she was grateful the few who had been there had taken such an interest in what she said.

I DIDN'T FEEL anything like that while I was giving the lecture. Somehow separated from the space around me, I kept thinking about my dream of being in the square outside the opera house, the phone call, her insistent voice, the hotel room and the oppressive hum of the air conditioning in the void before the telephone rang.

The next morning, my clothes had been wet. How strange. Maybe it was all true. Maybe it did happen.

I CLOSED my eyes for a moment to gather my thoughts and exhaustion swept over me. The magnificent parrot and her glass dark eyes flashed before me, like a freeze frame burned into my mind. She, the magnificent parrot, faded away and became the woman in the square, with her cold, controlling stare penetrating deep inside me. Her dark curls hanging down perfectly, framing her face and the perfect curve of her porcelain cheeks shining in the lights outside the opera house.

Juliet. Her name was Juliet. Did I not say that? It sounds improbable, doesn't it? Like something I made up. Maybe I want to project an idea of a woman dressed in untouched perfection, and perhaps Juliet, the cultural construct handed down from generation to generation from the pen of Shakespeare, fits the bill.

I doesn't really matter what she is called, though. You and I both know that. You've read the play, maybe seen it performed. You just need a name to hang her on, one that suits her and the situation. It's more so you'll know who she is when I next speak about her. Her name is not important, it is *she* who is important. She and her character, magnetic and dangerous, and her appearance, devastating.

Maybe I should have called her Helen.

But she was called Juliet.

I OPENED MY EYES, vowing to never close them again. Faces stared back at me. They had faces. That was reassuring. At the back of the room there was a space sectioned off, behind which was a desk, some equipment and a round-faced bald man in a t-shirt. He was in charge of the room from a technical standpoint.

Where was I in this temporary hierarchy?

Better not think about that.

He reminded me of someone, the man behind the desk.

The room was silent. The faces... I remembered why they were staring. I was standing in the middle of the floor between the audience and a desk placed on a raised platform we knew was supposed to represent a stage. There was a lectern next to it. That was for me. I glanced further along the desk on the stage and saw the session chair, to whom I'd said 'Thank you' and 'You're welcome'. He was looking at me curiously. He must have introduced me to the audience and they had been waiting for me to start.

I turned back to the audience and saw the round-faced bald man was looking at me too, so I started speaking.

I did not feel nervous any more. I was in a bubble of energy. Someone once told me... No, I once told someone, it is important to remember the audience, particularly at a conference, is not there to find fault or criticise. They are there to learn and to engage, and will do so whether you do well or not.

It doesn't matter too much how well you give the lecture, as you are not a public speaker, nor an actor, and no one is expecting that kind of performance. You are a professional, otherwise you wouldn't be giving the lecture, but only in the topic at hand. Imparting that professionalism and your accumulated knowledge is the point of the lecture. It is what you are there to do, as best as you can.

BUT I DIDN'T NEED to think about any of that. I was calm. The audience was over there in front of me, the session chair was presumably siting somewhere behind me, and there he was, the round-faced bald man at the desk behind the partition.

They say you should pick someone in the audience, maybe several people, and give the lecture to them. (Do they say that, or is it just me, now? I think they say that.) So I gave the lecture to him.

He still reminded me of someone. It took a while to narrow it down but eventually I settled on a Belgian man I had worked with who was extremely tall, had a perfectly round bald head, was a little overweight and had an infectious laugh. Yes, he reminded me very much of him.

But then I looked at someone in the audience, he turned and, as I glanced back the light flashed across his head, and I saw he was a sheep. That bald head, reflecting the light—wasn't human skin; it was curly white sheep fur.

How had I not spotted that before?

I watched in fascination as he reached with a hoof to fade the lights up a little, then shook his white furry head. I glanced away and could scarcely believe my eyes. The whole audience were sheep.

How had I...?

There must be something wrong.

Confused and unsure how to proceed, I turned to the session chair. I wanted to ask how so many sheep had been given passes to enter the conference, and why had they all come to see my presentation. But he smiled back at me so sweetly, so calmly, and with so much reassurance in his eyes, I wasn't worried anymore. He gestured at the audience as if to say to me 'You may carry on', and so I did.

For the most part, the sheep were attentive, which I thought impressive, apart from the odd bleat here and there, which I took for appreciation. They weren't wonderfully clean, I suppose; they did look as if they had just wandered in from a local field, although that seemed unlikely as we were in the middle of a large city and I didn't recall there being any open spaces nearby where a city farm could be housed.

It occurred to me they must, therefore, have managed to navigate the local transport system. I was thinking how developed and socialised they must be to have been able to understand the basic rights of passage that come with purchasing a ticket, as well as the abstract concepts inherent in monetary exchange. And that's not to mention their evident comprehension of maps and topographical layouts.

But all that was obvious, of course. They were sitting comfortably on chairs in a lecture theatre, listening to me speak. Simply, the registration process to get into the conference, choosing which talks to attend and then making their way to the theatre was evidence enough of their abilities.

None of them were rams, I noted. It relieved me somewhat. Having grown up in the countryside, I know how distracting they can be in a field full of ewes, even if it didn't say much for the gender distribution of my audience.

Maybe the organisers will mention that in their feedback about my lecture. They are always looking to increase the diversity of the audiences, but having an all-female audience is surely as lacking in diversity as having an all-male one, even if it inverts the centuries-old privilege us males have so long enjoyed.

. . .

WHILE I WAS SPEAKING, I remembered a walk I took in the countryside a year or so before, when I had gone back to my home town for my father's funeral. There is a huge reservoir near where we used to live, and my father would sometimes take me for walks along the water's edge, talking seriously with his head bowed, missing all the wildlife around us.

We always circulated the reservoir in the same direction, and so, on that cool summer's morning, I went the opposite way. I walked along the straight edge, where the view across the valley, patched in dark and light by the racing clouds, was at its most magnificent. The ground fell away steeply from the water's edge, down towards a farm nestled in a small wood. It must have been early summer, as the lambs were gambolling all around the older sheep with the bold and carefree energy of childhood.

Three lambs, sprayed in pink neon with the number of their mother, saw me walking along the path and ran straight up the hill towards me. They stood excitedly in front of me, stepping back and almost lying down on their front legs, like dogs, and wagging their tiny tails and looking up into my face, willing me to play with them.

I looked around and saw the older sheep, including two rams, watching me cautiously, but doing nothing. I could sense the meaning of their regard, that appeal from an adult to an adult to understand these are just children and they know not what they do.

I smiled and told the sheep everything was okay, I was simply going for a walk. And then I told the lambs I couldn't play, even though I would love to. I am not sure they understood. What child ever understands that you cannot play with them? I walked on, and the lambs followed me for a few paces before turning away and frolicking about among their elders.

I told someone that story, not that long ago, and they

asked me to wonder if it might be a metaphor for something. I told them then and I'll tell you now: if it is a metaphor, I have no idea for what.

THE LECTURE WAS OVER. I had reached the end of my slides. I cheated at the end and simply read out my conclusions rather than improvising something around them. I didn't have much hope of a response when I asked if there were any questions, although the sheep clapped their hooves together warmly. That's not to say I assumed the sheep were incapable of coming up with interesting points and starting a discussion. It's just that... well, with all their efforts in getting there in the first place, I thought they might be content simply to enjoy the lecture and leave it at that.

There were indeed no questions. I turned to watch the session chair give his closing remarks. I saw him speak, but the words didn't make it over to me. The audience applauded, and I turned back, impressed the sheep had once again been able to clap so effectively with their hooves. I was sure they lacked the equivalent of palms, on which we are so reliant to create and amplify that oh-so characteristic sound.

But when I turned back, I saw to my horror they were not sheep. They were people. Afraid and shaken, I was unable to tell whether they had been people all along and it was me who was... what? I didn't dare even think about that. But surely they couldn't *all* have been...?

Initially paralysed by fear, I then caught sight of the frightened face of the session chair. I panicked, grabbed my bag and walked as quickly as I could out of the lecture theatre without breaking into a run.

TWELVE

THE LIGHT IN THE PLAZA IS BLINDING. I HURRY ACROSS IT, BUT I can barely see. Light is coming at me from all directions, jabbing at me, insistent and sharp. It rains down from the skylights, bounces up from the floor, reflects off the metallic surfaces of the exhibition stands. I stumble, tripping over chairs and carpet squares, mumbling apologies through the harsh light that is blinding me.

I can't stop thinking about all those people staring back at me. Had they been there all along? But they were sheep, I was sure of it.

But what is knowing? What is surety?

I STUMBLE ON AND ON, for I don't know how long, until I reach the other side of the plaza. There is no bright light here, just stairs up to the entrance and then the outside world beyond.

I halt at the foot of the stairs. There are only a few steps, maybe six, but I am stuck. The entrance is not just a place of exit and entry, it is a space filled with other people, a stage, a theatre within a theatre in which a performance is expected, and I have to navigate it.

— But they don't know who you are, apart from by the name on your badge. They don't know *you*.

I am so relieved. It is my better, more worldly self. I don't even turn to look at him. I don't have to. I know he is there, at my shoulder. Smiling, almost smirking. I can feel his breath and the warm yet playful energy of his smile.

— Where have I been? I want to demand, but instead I think about what he is saying.

— They, those people in the entrance, they don't know you saw your entire audience turn into sheep right in front of your eyes.

That's true, I think. They don't.

— So you can walk right up there, right up to those people, then straight out the door and on to the street, and they won't know any different. They won't think you're going crazy because you saw twenty people turn into sheep and listen to your lecture, and then turn right back again once you'd finished. They'll think you are just as normal as they are.

I smile to myself. And who is to say they are so normal?

I almost say that out loud, but remember I don't have to do that for my better, more worldly self to know what I am saying. In any case, I don't have any time to lose. I have a plane to catch.

I shrug my shoulders, arranging the cloak of confidence my better, more worldly self has given me so it fits snugly on my frame. I'd better use it before it fades away and I'm trapped here at the bottom of the stairs forever.

I smile widely, ready for anyone who might see, a response or two to any question or comment quickly rehearsed in my mind. They'll see this smile, those people, and they'll know I'm norm... well, you get the idea.

I carefully place my foot on the first step and lift up my body. Then another. Then another. And then I forget what I am doing and, before I know it, I am in the entrance hall. I walk across it and no one notices me and stares, or tries to stop me.

I MAKE it to the door and, with an overwhelming sense of relief, I open it and walk through. In one fluid movement, I cast off my conference badge from around my neck, drop it into a bin by the entrance and let the warming sunlight strike me full in the face and lift my soul a quarter inch off the ground.

I hadn't noticed before, but there are people everywhere. Incomers and outgoers; hoverers and loiterers; faces and voices, some raised, others quiet; laughter and the occasional shout. Buses pass with roaring engines, and taxis too, crawling, beeping, with doors slamming, doors opening, boots opening, boots slamming. Boots and shoes on feet, walking around.

All those sounds and impressions clatter and bounce around the three-sided concrete box that makes up the floor, back wall and canopy of the entrance to the entrance. I am disorientated, thrown. The sun is no longer comforting and warming, but a line drawn across the sand separating here from there.

Down the stairs to the forecourt and the world beyond. Another roar as an engine pulls four wheels, a chassis, four doors, windows, a sour-faced driver and two passengers staring into space.

All three people presumably have a past, present and

future. It's your fancy as to what those might be, depending on your fondness for poetry.

WHAT AM I DOING? My better, more worldly self has gone and I am left in the lurch, swaying and trying to remember what I am supposed to do now.

I have to go to the airport.

Good, good. It's good to have that thought fixed in my mind. It's not urgent I get there but I may as well go now. I step forward, further away from the entrance and towards the clattering, bouncing sounds. Steeling myself, I walk straight over to the nearest taxi. The driver is leaning over with one hand on the passenger seat so he can see me and the better hear what I have to say.

I look at him and try to speak but nothing comes out. He tries to understand me, cocking his head to one side, but decides he cannot follow me and looks at me strangely.

— Where did you…

But before I can hear what he has to say, someone approaches and speaks to me. I don't recognise him but he seems to know me. I don't understand why he is accosting me.

I straighten up and shake my head to realign my thoughts. I see a man, a young man, crossing the road. He turns slightly towards me to check if there is any traffic coming and my heart stops. The day crashes down around me and there is the opera house, there is the statue, pointing at Don Giovanni, and the music screaming into my soul.

It *is* him. From last night but not from last night, from so many nights ago. My friend who died, when none of us could have believed it. My friend who was gone long ago. And there he is, exactly as he was twenty years ago. It is not someone who looks like him; it is not an apparition or my imagination. It *is* him.

I am in my hotel room, knowing I need answers. I am in the square outside the opera house. I am in her eyes, cold and compelling, and I am in the rain and the reflections. And I know, I know, I know what she said and I can't escape it even though I don't want it to be true.

I SPIN AWAY from the taxi, which I don't think is even there anymore. I look down at my hands and realise they are empty. One of them should have the handle of a suitcase inside its palm, and I turn, confused. I look around frantically but my friend is no longer there. I glance back to the entrance, with its clattering and bouncing sounds.

My suitcase. I don't have my suitcase.

I panic, wondering where it is. I put my hand in my jacket pocket and pull out a receipt from the cloakroom. I have a flashback to another time entirely, before the bouncing light and the blank faces and the coffee and the calm energy of the lecture theatre, and I remember I checked my suitcase into the cloakroom.

But that means I must have wheeled it all the way from the hotel. Yet I have no recollection of that at all. I remember the mother and her pram, the taxi driver and the shut coffee shop, but at no point along that trajectory of memories is the sound of a suitcase being trundled along a pavement and the draw of its weight on my arm.

Up the stairs, to the entrance. That's it, get your suitcase.

But they won't let me in. A big man with a flat head and no expression blocks my way. I tell him I have my suitcase in there, that I need it, it's mine, I have to get it back and I need to go to the airport.

— Badge.

— I had it, just now.

— Badge.

— I just came out of here, straight past you. I threw my badge into the bin straight after I walked out.

— No badge, no entry.

BEFORE I GO on to describe my rising panic and the terrible, terrible worry that I hadn't really been... no, surely I was actually at the conference?

Before I talk about that, I should take a moment here to explain that this man, my interlocutor, was not inarticulate, despite his apparently limited vocabulary. Or I assume he wasn't.

The issue we both had in continuing our conversation was there were people coming in and out of the entrance constantly, him checking their badges and thus being distracted and relying on the economy of pragmatic mono-syllabic communication. On the other hand, there was me, continually having to step back out of the way of yet another person, and so not having the opportunity to present my case via the kind of constructive narrative that would have persuaded him of my veracity and authenticity.

Or I assume it would. That interaction, I later realised after much reflection, also wanted for the lack of nonverbal communication, us not being able to concentrate on each other.

Not only that but I was profoundly disturbed by having just seen my dead friend, the emotional turmoil of his loss once more overwhelming me, alongside the awful sense everything that had passed the previous evening was clearly not a dream or nightmare that could be allowed simply to fade away.

I was nevertheless sufficiently conscious of my need to

obtain my suitcase that I was able to suppress those feelings. And, if I say so myself, I was doing a fairly good job of projecting imploring sincerity. I am sure, in different circumstances, it would have moved the doorman emotionally, perhaps to the extent he would have reconsidered his implacability and, I would like to think, let me retrieve my suitcase even in the absence of my badge.

BUT IT DIDN'T HAPPEN that way. I became frustrated and angry. I told him he must remember me, that I had come in via that entrance and left by the same one, right in front of his face. He asked me what I had done with my badge. I told him I had thrown it in that bin, gesturing to the floor beside me, but there was no bin.

I realised later it could have been a temporary bin, one that may have, in the time between me throwing away my badge and returning to fetch my suitcase, been removed for emptying. But I am sure you are well aware by now I was not able to think clearly anymore and such rationality would not have occurred to me. Instead, I panicked and tried to push past the implacable doorman with the flat head. He pushed me back, and it was then I noticed the session chair, the one who was so reassuring and calm, walking out of the building.

I called out for him to help me, but either he didn't hear me or he ignored me, as he carried on walking down the steps and then up the road, presumably to his hotel. I watched him leave and felt lost and alone. I turned to the doorman and angrily tried to push past him, telling him he was an idiot.

He must have alerted a colleague, as two hands like slabs of meat slid up my armpits and, with my shoulders pinned back, I was hauled down the stairs by an unknown man. I lost my balance and fell like a rag doll. His breath, laboured

THIRTEEN

I WAS INITIALLY RELIVED TO SEE THE POLICE. I THOUGHT THEY would listen to me, that they would want to get to the bottom of the situation and sort it out. But they saw me simply as another foreigner causing a nuisance, a public nuisance at that. They had no interest in listening.

Of course, they didn't speak much English, at least the officers who arrested me didn't, so I couldn't communicate very well with them. But I suspect it might have been the same even if everyone had spoken English well. I simply could not get my words out.

Not that I was afforded much time to say anything. Once my grunting, rasping restrainer had let go of me, the policemen twisted my arms behind my back and handcuffed me. They turned me around to push me into the police car, and I saw everyone, people from the conference, some who I knew, staring at me. Some in disbelief, some in shock and some in judgement.

What about the doorman? He was back at his post, unruffled, acting as if nothing had happened. Maybe to him, it was all nothing. Perhaps I would be transformed into an anecdote

for his wife later that evening, or for his friends at the local
bar. The grunting, rasping man, or the person I presumed
him to be, was already walking back up the steps, straight-
ening his jacket over his massive frame.

I was alone.

My life fell away from me and an overwhelming fear shot
through me.

I was scared.

THE DOOR of the police car closed and I knew nothing was in
my control. All my fanciful thinking, all my paranoia, all my
theories and my expectations, everything Juliet had said
solidified into the reality of the bars on the metal grill that
separated me from the front of the police car.

This is real. It is not a dream. Now is the present, in this
moment. And what if every single person around me was an
android fashioned from other people's memories?

IT IS SAID that an electron exists in two states. One is as a
particle, a fixed point in relation to the nucleus of an atom.
The other is as a wave, a theoretical point one could call a
cloud of positivity where, to all intents and purposes, the
electron exists at all points in the cloud or wave at the same
time, thus surrounding the nucleus. A nucleus, that is, that
remains generally stable as long as the number of neutrons
and protons is in accord.

I had been living in that positively charged electron cloud,
circulating, undulating around the nucleus, flirting with it,
one could say, trying not to be pinned down and become a
particle, a fixed point.

What was the nucleus? That was the core of me. The
nucleus of reality. That was the part of me that interacted

with the real world; the condensed part, the part that could be pinpointed. And the rest? That cloud-wave was the place where I resided, apart from myself, making up the whole but separated. It was the conscious me, associated with but not integral to the body that connected me to the outside world.

The cloud, charged and floating, had become bigger and bigger, taking me further and further away from the nucleus. I had lost touch with reality.

I had enjoyed that, I suppose. It was more interesting than the cold boredom of the day to day. But perhaps I had drifted too far from the coalesced, solid part of me. It, that nucleus of reality, seemed to have shrunk, or at least become less and less relevant, less and less my centre of gravity. The cloud-wave had more energy than the nucleus. That, surely, is unstable?

AND THEN THE door of the police car slammed and the extra charge dissipated and the electron became a fixed point. There were no blank faces in that car, no sheep, no blinding lights, no feathers and no glass dark eyes staring back at me.

There was a metal grill between the back seat and the two policemen who sat up in the front. There were short hairs growing on the backs of their necks. I estimated they had had a haircut on the same day, maybe even at the same time, during a break from duty, and now the tiny hairs had begun to regrow after being shaved to square off the classic policeman style.

The difference between the two of them was: a) the hairs were of a different colour, the driver's hairs being dusty grey and the passenger's hairs a reddy blond; and b) the skin on the back of the driver's neck was red, or more purple-red, and reminded me of a turkey I had seen recently on a news item on farming, whereas the other had a soft, plump and pink neck, like gammon, swollen with the fat of too much fast food. Perhaps their necks were a before-and-after ensemble, a cautionary tale for anyone considering a life in the police force.

The car smelled as if it hadn't been cleaned in a good long while. Or perhaps a previous occupant had been a little loose with his contents. I sat up off the seat, having remembered I had only got this suit back from the dry cleaners two days before I took my flight.

I think about that memory sometimes, when I want to ponder how the human brain is capable of distracting itself in moments of high stress, and how one's preoccupations shift with one's shifting circumstances. It is, in fact, my favourite memory of the journey. It sits between bleak suppositions about the gravity, and vulnerability, of my situation, and the fear that what Juliet had told me about dark forces slowly replacing the human race could all be true.

Perhaps I was being taken away to prevent me taking part in the uprising to save us from total destruction.

THE DESK SERGEANT was not unkind. The two police officers who had arrested me finally looked at me, once I had been checked in and told to wait on the bench.

They stared at me curiously.

I had several theories about that look. Some of the theories were created to massage my ego, which was somewhat bruised, while others confirmed my darkest fears. All the while, my mind flashed back to the steps up to the entrance of the conference centre and seeing all those people—my colleagues, my peers, my seniors—staring at me like I was a circus freak. I dared not even think at the time what the consequences could be for my job and my career.

— Although you did deliver the lecture and had a good response, so it wasn't all bad.

That was him. My better, more worldly self. He popped over to say that, and then disappeared. I found his arrival unwanted and his instant departure somewhat irritating. He might have stayed to help me, or at least to advise me. Otherwise what's the point in making a mocking statement disguised as helpful encouragement?

HOW LONG DID I wait there on that bench? I don't know. I don't wear a watch, and even if I had at the time, the police would have taken it off me.

Had they taken my personal effects by that point? It doesn't matter. It's not going to change your understanding of my predicament if I get minor details like that right or wrong. Not that you could check. It's all simply to give the right impression, even if the recall can be a little hazy.

There was probably a clock on the wall. I should have made a note of the time.

I don't know long I sat there on the bench, watching the comings and goings of the police. My arresting officers left again at some point, presumably to go back on the beat. I waited there long enough for that.

And then I was called in to be interviewed. You could say it was presented more like an informal chat than an interrogation. The officer gave me the impression he simply wanted to know what had happened. I was initially relieved to find he spoke excellent English, but in some ways it only made things worse.

I TOLD him I had forgotten to take my suitcase with me when I had left the conference hall, having given my lecture a few minutes earlier, and when I tried to go back in, the doorman wouldn't let me. I had thrown away my badge, I explained, without thinking and the man on the door had not wanted to help me or listen to my story.

I sounded reasonable, straightforward, believable. I thought so, anyway, and so did the police officer. Or he gave that impression. He nodded in silence in a way that seemed to say he understood me, not just literally, but on a more fundamental level; that he empathised with me. He made notes, he underlined, he drew a circle around a word. He got up. I looked up at his lined face, his drooping moustache and his sagging eyes, and I smiled as sweetly as I could.

He regarded me for a moment, and then, before turning on his heel and leaving, he asked me where I had been staying, what my suitcase looked like and what was inside it. My heart jumped with a little flutter, by which I am trying to indicate I started to, finally, feel as if I was being believed and it would only be a matter of time before all this bother was straightened out and I could go home. Okay, I'd missed my flight, but there'd be others. I'd rather get this sorted first and leave with everything cleared up.

Then I was alone in the room and the happiness and expectation and confidence seeped out of me. The walls were cold and hard now, as was the table, and the cold, hard thrum of the air conditioning rattled my mind.

I was alone in theory only, of course. In reality there was the abstract presence of the video camera and what lay beyond its glass eye. (She, it) stared at me, a single eye, a cyclops, from behind the wall; cold and penetrating, observing from a space unknown and unknowable. It was a reminder of permission and exclusion, of where the line is drawn and the shifting nature of trespass. (She, it) stared at me (the video camera is a she, don't ask me why, although you've probably already guessed), a single eye coldly regarding me.

THEY FIXED THE TYPEWRITER, by the way. It was a small part they needed, nothing complicated. But we do not have the means of manufacture here and it took a few days to arrive.

Oh, but of course. You know the typewriter was fixed, otherwise I couldn't have…

THE DOOR OPENED. The officer who I had spoken to before came back with a colleague, a dishevelled man in an old, ill-fitting suit I assumed he had worn to work every day since he had bought it, probably second hand in a charity shop.

His hair was clean and combed, however, which made me think the suit was an affectation to give the impression he was causal and not at all like these uniformed boys with their square haircuts and neat ties. And he was as thin as a rake, with smooth, clean skin. No fatty deposits, no bulging neck. I wondered if he might be vegetarian.

I didn't ask who he was, but he told me he was the station doctor. The officer had brought him along for a chat, apparently.

— Why?

I asked myself that question, and then I asked it out loud.

Ignored, the question hung in the air until the doctor had made himself comfortable. He looked me straight in the eye and said, again in excellent English, it was all just routine; he was here for a chat and there was nothing to worry about.

That depends on which side of the table you are sitting, matey.

. . .

I DID NOT EXIST. Not in a conventional paper-and-documents kind of way. Or that is what the officer told me. I got a bit frustrated at this point. I reminded him I had a flight to catch and if they were not intending pressing charges, then I would like to leave, suitcase or no suitcase, and go home.

A pretty little speech it was, too, but the officer did not reply. Instead, he went on insisting I did not exist. He told me there was no record of me at the conference, there was no suitcase of my description left in the cloakroom, and no one could find the lecture I had apparently given on the programme. He had checked with the session chair, but he'd said he had been held up in traffic and hadn't made it to the conference in time for his session.

I thought of mentioning the round-faced bald technician at the back of the room, but then I remembered he turned into a sheep and thought better of it. In any case, there wasn't time to chip in because the officer was also telling me there was no record of my having been booked on to the flight home. There was no record of my arrival into the city, or of me staying at the hotel.

— Why did you come to our city?

He spoke from somewhere outside the dark lake of my mind, where my thoughts were sinking into oblivion and the air was bleeding. I presume it was the officer who spoke. I looked up at the doctor, who smiled at me as if everything was perfectly fine and there was nothing to worry about.

My throat was thick and my tongue was heavy. I glanced across at the policeman, who had assumed stock concerned expression no. 42 from the police academy handbook of official facial positions.

— I don't... I don't understand, I stammered out.

I stared at the table between us, unsure what to do or think. I remembered the magnificent white dove, her shimmering feathers and glass bright eyes, and my heart ached.

What was happening to me? I looked up at the video camera. (She, it) stared at me with her cyclops eye. I saw the line between permission and exclusion was drawn within myself, that there was a place within myself where I could not know what I had done or where I had been. A place where I was a secret from myself.

I saw in her cyclops eye there was not just my better, more worldly self, but another entire version of me, acting and thinking without my knowledge and against myself. Was he the one observing me and controlling me?

— I am going to leave you now. Why don't you have a chat with the doctor?

I stared at the doctor, then watched with horror as the policeman got up and walked out. I understood now how they saw me, and what that would mean for me, and panic rose up within me. I fleetingly wondered if one or both of them were androids, but I knew what was coming next was far, far worse than that.

The doctor considered me for a moment or two, and then, with the slow, inevitable fall of words like the tolling of a bell, asked me how I was feeling.

FOURTEEN

I TRIED TO RESIST HIM, THE DOCTOR. I KNEW HE WANTED TO know what was going on in my mind, but I also knew I didn't want to tell him. I was sure of that. How could I know he wouldn't use my thoughts against me?

But he was kind and straightforward and made everything seem okay. That's how they get you, you know. And I was very tired all of a sudden and it occurred to me I hadn't spoken to anyone about any of this. Not to someone who I could trust.

Who would I have spoken to? My father, perhaps. But he had died and I was all alone. Yes, my friends had said they were there for me, but they had families and I knew there was only so much they could do. What was I compared to their children? They didn't really have the time to spare, and only so much attention they could give.

I knew that and they knew that, and I saw a kind of sadness in their eyes when they looked at me, as if they could see there was so much more to talk about; that I needed so much more help than they could give; that I was lost. But I was not their responsibility and I had to handle this on my own.

I DON'T KNOW how or why exactly, but my father's death had unanchored me. We hadn't been particularly close, but there was something between us. To move from the atomic metaphor I employed previously to a boating one, in the police car I had felt unstable, nebulous, floating, dissipated. Now, here, in the quiet of the police interview room, with only the faint hum of the air conditioning, the cyclops eye staring at me and the doctor smiling while he reached down into my soul, I was no longer a cloud. I was adrift on a vast ocean, with no land in sight. The rope that tethered me had perished or been cut and there was nothing to which I could anchor myself.

I hope you understand what I mean.

If I could describe the metaphor a little further, the water is not stormy, but with long, thick, undulating waves, like oil. Not threatening, but enough to remind me I was not in control and there were forces outside of me operating within my soul.

Who was I?

I no longer knew.

EMOTION, that emotion, the one I didn't want to have, crashed over me and I cried. I told myself I was exhausted.

— Why don't you tell me what happened?

I stared at him. — When?

— Whenever you think is important.

I frowned. I didn't really understand what he meant.

— Did you really come here to go to a conference?

— Yes, I said indignantly. Then I remembered what the police officer had told me. — Yes, I repeated quietly.

And then I remembered my bag. It must have bits and pieces from the conference inside. And my laptop. It had my presentation on it, and the emails from the conference organisers inviting me, confirming my registration, discussing my lecture. I was elated.

— My laptop. It's all on there. You can see everything. That will prove what I'm saying is true.

The doctor tilted his head and regarded me.

— The police are looking at your laptop. They prefer to do that themselves.

— But I can show them everything. How will they be able to get in if they don't have the password? How will they know where to look?

— If they need your assistance, I'm sure they'll ask.

I sighed, deflated. I had entertained the idea that, in a blink, we would open my laptop, I would show them I had indeed been registered at the conference. They would then realise it had all been a terrible mix-up and I would finally get to go home.

— Why don't you tell me what happened?

I HAVE to say at this point, I don't really know why I am recording this conversation in such detail. I find it fairly boring and predictable so far. Don't you?

I have talked with *them* about why I focus on it so much, why I am writing so much about it. *They* suggested it's because it's the first time I admitted out loud, and by extension to myself, what had been going on and how I had been feeling about myself.

I am not so sure that is the only reason. *They* do like to try to find a single explanation for things, to make it easy to characterise a moment or pivot point. But I find their ideas sometimes a little reductive.

I *was* tired, exhausted even, and I *was* lost and alone on my ocean, and it *was* the first time I'd admitted to myself I needed some help to re-anchor myself. But there are other reasons why I focus on this moment so much.

Juliet had been the only person with whom I had discussed my fears, and I had known instinctively they were not of the kind I should share with anyone else. And if her explanation was true, and the people of the world were indeed being replaced with androids by a dark force hell bent on world domination, then…, then…

It was then I had the epiphany, the icy realisation.

There, in that room, in front of that kind doctor, I under-stood finally the implications of what I had seen and Juliet had explained to me. If the people I saw from the past really were androids taking the place of humans, then how many other people, copied from the minds of humans the world over, were fakes? What proportion of the people I saw when I walked down the street, when I took a train, when I sat in a café, when I ate lunch, when I walked in the park or visited a gallery? When—and this was the part that made my heart sink—I was in the conference earlier that day, how many of the people there were not in fact human, but were androids, simply filling in the gaps?

What about when I got my coffee that morning from the exhibition stand? How many of the delegates milling around without faces were androids? How many of the sheep in the audience? The round-faced bald man behind the desk? The other people on the steps outside the conference centre? Was that why the session chair did not respond when I called out to him? Had he been replaced by an android after my lecture? And when I was being pushed into the police car and all those people were staring at me? How many of them were androids?

I STARE at the doctor suspiciously.

— Is there anything you would like to tell me? the doctor asks kindly but firmly, like a teacher who knows you have done something wrong.

I stare at him and think about what Juliet said, about what it means. The androids are simply filler, background, so we do not notice the humans are being replaced, which means the few people with whom we interact are the only real ones left. And that implies, as long as someone talks to me, they must be a real human.

This doctor sitting in front of me, he must be a real human, right? He is, isn't he?

I sit back in my chair and regard him, inspect him.

— Are you really human?

I instantly regret asking out loud.

— I think so, as far as I can tell. I suppose René Descartes would have something to say about that. How about you?

I almost laugh, but stop myself in time. Of course I am human, I want to say, to cry out. I want to mock him for apparently not knowing the bald (round-faced?) truth, but I can see this is not the time.

— Why do you ask? He softens his expression. I stare back at him, unsure what to say next. — Have you had any reason to doubt whether the people you see around you are real human beings?

I smile involuntarily. I want to ask him, 'Haven't you, every day since you were born?', but I remember that is not the subject of the interview.

— They told me you met a woman last night, in the square outside the opera house. I think it was a patrol car that spotted you, and then of course there is the CCTV. Does that have any connection with what happened today?

My blood runs cold. So I *am* under surveillance. Maybe she is too. I panic for her, hoping she is safe.

— It's okay, you can trust me. Anything you say is strictly between us. I am here to help you. I just want to understand.

Isn't it strange? Maybe not strange per se, but certainly interesting that one person can say something to you and it has one effect, while someone else could say exactly the same thing and the effect is entirely different. If most people had uttered those words to me, I would simply have brushed them off and changed the subject.

If we think about the context, there I was in the police interview room, having been arrested, and in ordinary circumstances that would have left me prickly and embarrassed and, as I would say now, in need of reasserting my agency in my own life to take back some sense of control. (And there is nothing like sitting in a cage in the back of a police car to make you feel powerless. It is, I am sure, as much a part of the philosophy behind its design as for the protection of the police officers sitting up front.)

And I did feel those things, to a certain extent. But superseding that, I was desperate and afraid, and acutely aware of being vulnerable and alone. Plus, there was something so disarming about the simplicity of the way the doctor spoke. I know it's all part of the training, but I had the sense I really could tell him anything and not be judged.

I am saying that because there is a part of me, especially now, that wishes I could have held out and not told him about Juliet and the dark forces, and the long lost-friends I had seen in different places. I wish I had never mentioned my father and how isolated and adrift I was, but I couldn't help myself. Once I started talking, it all came out. I checked the police tape wasn't running, but the cyclops eye was watching me, and I don't think I could have stopped myself even if they had been recording me.

I wish I hadn't mentioned how lonely and adrift I was. It made him think it was the main issue. Once I said that, he stopped asking me about Juliet and androids, and he kept talking about that, and the words flowed and flowed out of me and I couldn't control myself anymore. Then I cried and I wish and I wish I could have stopped myself. Maybe if I had, I could have avoided what came next. But there was something about the simplicity of the way he spoke.

HE ASKED me if it wouldn't be better if I stayed the night at the police station.

It was already late and there was nowhere for me to go now, and I didn't know what to say so I just mumbled something, and he called back in the police officer, or it could have been another one, and then I was at the front desk filling in forms and I knew I was slipping down a deep well, further and further down, under the dark water, and there was a huge weight on me and a heaviness in the air and it was pushing down on my head and my shoulders and my chest, and I could barely lift my arm to sign the forms, and they took my fingerprints and my picture, and they took my jacket and my belt and my laces from my shoes, and I wondered what on earth they were doing until a nice police-woman with a belt around her waist and laces in her shoes took me to a cold cell and I walked in and my heart sank further than it ever had done when I saw the built-in metal toilet and the hard bench and the thin blanket and the tiny, high window and the walls that shone as if they'd just been painted, and she explained and explained and I tried to listen, but my mind stopped working and I was trying not to be there anymore, and the big metal door that I must have passed through closed behind me and I knew I was truly alone, alone, alone in that cold room, and I looked down at my shoes, which were yawning open, and I looked at my hands, and I looked at the loops on the waistband of my trousers, and I looked at my hands, and I realised why they had taken my jacket and my belt and my laces and I realised what they thought I might do to myself and what they thought of me, and I finally saw how far I had fallen, down into the dark well so far I couldn't see out any more, and I cried, not because I wanted to, but because I couldn't stop myself, and maybe it was tiredness, but it was mostly grief and hatred and sorrow and frustration and the knowledge I was breaking apart and at the bottom of the dark well there was always a police cell, and I knew although I may one day do the same things again in the same places with the same people as I had done before, I would never be the same again.

I would never be the same again.

MUCH LATER, I thought about Juliet, and I stopped crying and wondered what was happening to me. I was frightened so I put the thin blanket over my shoulders and rocked back and forth, but it didn't warm me up because the cold was coming from within.

FIFTEEN

THE THING I WILL ALWAYS REMEMBER ABOUT THE PLACE I ended up after that is the light. The light had a clarity there. I don't know when I first became aware of it. Not at the beginning. I don't think I was capable of appreciating it at the beginning.

Everything from the time I arrived is a haze, a dark mess. I can never sift through the jumble of memories, impressions, feelings and dreams from that period enough to be able to construct any kind of meaningful narrative, let alone understand what it all meant. I am aware of some things that happened at the beginning, of course, awful things, terrible flashes, images, sensations and smells emanating from the darkness, but they are disconnected, abstract, isolated.

I don't know how long that period lasted, but I do know that, one day, I saw a light, and it was full of clarity. It might have been outside in the gardens, or maybe it was in the common room, the one with the tall windows. No matter. What I do remember is I turned a corner and there it was, a beautiful bright light that seemed to bathe everything in calm. A beautiful bright light that shimmered through the morning trees.

Or maybe it *was* in the common room. The windows were very tall. Or was it a wall made of glass blocks? The glass blocks, if there were any, scattered the light to such an extent it became diffuse, almost cloud-like, and everything seemed white, perfectly white, with the slightest hint of blue that reminded me of washing powder adverts from my childhood.

Your whites brighter.

Daz. They meant 'dazzle', didn't they? That occurred to me just now. When I was a child, I had a friend called Darren, who was known as Daz. Or was he a character on television? I don't recall having any friends when I was a child, so maybe he was.

No matter. Daz, the washing powder, was Darren to me, and I always assumed the washing powder had been named after someone called Darren, perhaps its inventor. But now I see Daz is short for dazzle.

That hint of blue was to make the white seem even whiter, to make it almost clinical in its purity. But it made the colour fade in the rest of your clothes.

I don't think I knew anyone called Darren.

Not then, and not now.

When I dream about that place, about the light that was full of clarity, the dream always starts in Barcelona. I know it is Barcelona, initially instinctively, and then later I recognise I am in that city. I am there for a conference. I don't think I am speaking there, not in the dream. I never speak in my dreams, or never out loud; I simply think things and they become known by the other participants. Is that strange?

I'm not speaking at the conference, I know that. In my dream, the conference is always at the Gran Fira, the big venue on the way out of town towards the airport. It's located on a corner, set back from the road on a piece of concrete that is always hot underfoot. The weather is hot, but I don't feel it in my dream.

I am already inside the conference hall, walking around looking for where I should be. The giant space in the hall is divided into 'rooms' by huge grey curtains hanging down from the ceiling. Part-way along the curtains are temporary doors that allow access to what is now called a room even though it's just a square of space on the ground.

I am walking around, lost. I end up behind one of those temporary rooms and watch the flowing of the grey curtains in the airwaves caused by the air conditioning. The curtains look like the surface of a slowly undulating sea.

I ONCE TOOK a ferry from Lowestoft to Zeebrugge and the sea was grey, solid and implacable; flowing, undulating, pitching the boat gently. A boat that had been so huge when I stood next to it in the docks, but now was dwarfed by the splendid infinity of nature. The clouds were magnificent towers, or more like ships, perhaps floating castles.

The piercing sunlight reached down to the sea between them and I understood why we, by which I mean humans, have assumed that there are heavenly beings, gods, controlling our lives. What a comforting thought it seemed when I was on the boat, watching the sun reaching down to the sea, illuminating patches of water gold in the grey seascape.

. . .

I FOLLOW the line of the undulating grey curtains and find a long, low corridor that leads towards a bright white space. I don't know what the space is or where it will take me, but I am compelled to follow the reflections on the highly polished floor that seem to draw me on and on, step by step, further and further towards the bright light. The conference is far behind me now. I am glad because it has been bothering me and made me stressed. I needed to escape. I know that now.

At the end, the corridor opens out into a long, open white space with windows from floor to ceiling. The light streams through the windows and reflects off every surface. It is so bright, it initially blinds me, but, as my eyes adjust, I see it isn't the large room in the Gran Fira behind the conference; it is the common room, with its huge windows or wall made of glass blocks. There are books everywhere, many tattered, many covered in writing and doodles, and I am standing on the threshold, nervous like it's the first day at school.

Everyone is there and it all seems so complete, like a picture, and I don't see how I could fit into a picture that is already complete. So I stand there and gaze at the bright light and the bright room, so full of clarity.

I want to run away from the brightness, from the clarity, from that place, from myself, but I know I can't because there is no escape. And anyway, *they* tell me again and again and again there would be no point. The only way to leave is when you are ready.

They say that in reality, but not in the dream. In the dream, that is not said, but I know it has been said and I know it is true. That is clarity.

IT HAS TAKEN me a long time to realise this: I do not think it was an entirely bad idea that I stayed there. I see now I clearly needed some rest. I needed a break, and not in the weekend getaway, romantic mini-break-for-two sense, and not in the two weeks by the pool in an all-inclusive resort with a happy hour from four till eight sense, and certainly not in the four weeks trekking in Kathmandu sense. Nor in the staycation watching films and pretending to sort your life out sense. Nor in any other sense other than that I needed a break from everything, including from the responsibility of looking after myself.

I could have said I needed a break from myself, and maybe would have said that at some point, but I know I didn't need that. It was to spend more time with myself, with no distractions, that I needed.

You see, I was listening. It all sank in eventually.

THERE WAS a lot of clarity in what *they* said. Maybe that's why I saw the light that way on that day. I guess it took a few weeks, but I started to see things a little more clearly. And I stopped thinking about other things and what had been happening to me. I was embarrassed to recall what had seemed so completely real to me only a few weeks before.

No more magnificent parrot, no more magnificent dove, although I wouldn't have minded seeing the latter, if I'm honest. *They* suggested the white and black birds represented two sides of the same coin, two facets of the same idea. I suggested in turn that their analysis was a little simplistic and perhaps the issue was more complex than that.

I suppose I was offended.

They suggested simplistic or even clichéd ways of looking at things are sometimes employed by the subconscious to flag up ideas and concepts and present them in a digestible and relatable way for the conscious mind to process.

I suggested in turn that perhaps they were missing the

point. I didn't mean the metaphor was simplistic and I preferred a more complicated explanation for the appearance of two birds, one black, one white, but rather I found the idea they were a metaphor presented by my subconscious brain to highlight something to my conscious mind as itself a little simplistic.

— You mean you think the birds were real? one of them asked, trying to sound incredulous.

I admit I was a little uncomfortable at having that notion presented back to me out loud and I attempted to launch into an explanation of the way in which the perception of reality differs from reality itself. But even I knew I was splitting hairs, so I let the subject drop.

I could have said: — I know what I saw.

But they knew as well as I that the question actually was: — Do I really know what I saw?

It's all about perception.

I perceived they were beginning to come to some rather uncomfortable conclusions about me, so I told them it was all a misunderstanding about the two birds and I hadn't realised initially what they meant by their suggestion.

I had to say that. After all, what self-respecting man of my age, experience and standing in life could admit to having seen people turn in front of his very eyes into a magnificent parrot and a magnificent dove? That would to be tantamount to admitting... well, you get the idea.

WHO ARE YOU?

You, I mean. The 'you' reading this page.

Who are you?

I have been addressing you, both obliquely and directly, for some time now, and yet I am not sure I have a clear idea of who 'you' are.

. . .

THEY ASKED ME THAT, about who I am addressing in writing this. During one of our chats.

— Who are you writing this for?

— Well…

I started to respond, thinking I knew the answer, but it turned out I hadn't thought about it enough in concrete terms to be able to say who exactly.

But you, reading this, are me, right? You must be. I am writing this for me, aren't I?

I don't mean my better, more worldly self, of course. It's not that he knows everything. He was *in absentia* for much of what happened, so he actually could do with reading it. But he would claim to be uninterested. He doesn't read books, in any case, and he certainly is not going to start by reading one about me. Although I'm sure he would read it behind my back. That cool thing is just an act, you know.

No, this isn't for him. The you I am addressing is the quietest version of me. The one who I am when I am calm, at home, content with the world, happy to be alone, reading a book and occasionally looking out of the window to reflect and piece things together. The one who can drink just one glass of wine and be satisfied; who doesn't solicit company, but is happy to have it; who goes to bed at a reasonable hour and wakes up refreshed and ready for the day.

I wish I were you more often. You are the best of me. And I am writing this for you. You deserve an explanation.

WHEN I STOOD at the threshold of the common room, not knowing how I could fit into the picture, someone came over to me. He was like me, as in he was staying there, although he was not like me because he had been there a long time and he had found his place in the picture.

He came over and invited me into the light. I'll be honest with you, I thought he seemed a little crazy at first, but I soon realised he was the sanest person I had ever met. He was filled with so much clarity.

SIXTEEN

IT OCCURRED TO ME THE OTHER DAY, WHEN I WAS WAITING FOR the delivery of yet another ribbon for the typewriter, that I didn't say how I ended up in that place, the place where I found clarity.

And when I started thinking about that, it occurred to me there are a lot of things I have not explained.

I think there are many reasons for that.

The simplest, and least interesting, explanation is I don't want to because I am trying to hide things, even if it is from myself. Another might be I am embarrassed about what happened. Maybe the you reading this isn't a version of me but someone else entirely who happens to have obtained these papers, and so I subconsciously want to limit the possibility of you being able to trace it all back to me, the one who actually lived through it all.

I could be doing it because I want to protect the innocent, as they say. I could also being doing it because I still believe those dark forces are still out there, looking for any clues to track down anyone who knows about the plot to replace the human race with androids and eliminate them before word gets out.

Maybe I want to protect the reputation of my boss and the company where I worked. Not because I harbour hopes of ever returning, but because they were involved only incidentally and so why should they become tarnished with my brush?

I WAS REPATRIATED. That's how I got back.

The police dropped all charges against me in the end. It turned out they had spelled my name wrong when they were checking up on me. So of course they didn't have a trace of me at the conference or anywhere in the city. I settled my hotel bill, but it was too late to halt the inevitable. The conversation with the police doctor had ensured that.

I suppose it would have happened one way or another.

THEY TOOK me back under escort, with someone waiting for me at the other end. It was both humiliating and ridiculous. I suppose it wasn't all bad, though, as I was completely detached from myself.

There was the physical me being taken to the airport, taken through security and boarded on to the plane, with all those people looking at me and the guards on either side, and then there was my experience of it, which was at least once removed from the actual events. It wasn't exactly an out-of-body experience, but I certainly did not experience any of it in a direct manner.

It was a little like how I imagine it might be for participants on reality television. There but not there, present in the space but with the knowledge that *you* are not there. It's not you on the screen. It's a copy of yourself, a display model.

Not that I watch television, nor ever really have. I do realise almost everyone says that, but in my case it's true.

THERE WAS a television in the common room, but it was a rare occasion when there was something on I wanted to watch. Sometimes there was a film I like, but mostly I read. I caught up on a lot of books while I was there, although I confess I found the selection in what one might call the library rather under-stimulating. I can't help wondering if it might have been on purpose.

I liked to read in the common room, even if there was a film showing. It was sometimes distracting having it on in the background, especially if it was stimulating and it wound up the audience. They did enjoy throwing themselves into the story, it has to be said. But I found the energy of those moments somehow comforting, especially for not partici-pating directly.

ONE DAY, I took a walk in the garden. I don't mean it was the first time I had walked in the garden. I had done that often, once I felt comfortable being outside again.

I mean one day, I took a walk in the garden and it felt different. Everything, in fact, felt different from any other walk I had ever taken up until that point.

Of course, that happens with the changing seasons, even with each new day. The weather changes, the plants grow or die back, the trees come into leaf, the birds come and go as winter slides into spring, then summer. That and the ever-changing populations of insects. The humidity in the air is different, the luminosity, the intensity of the shade. The hum as the bees search the flowers for nectar, or the cold rustling of the winter branches.

And we become different. The garden may be the same from one day to the next, and the words we use may stay the same, but the way we think about and perceive it changes with our shifting moods.

And over time, we change, sometimes imperceptibly, sometimes noticeably, but always just enough to feel different, leaving us struck with the sensation that we are in a new place. A new person in a new place.

We have difficulties in expressing that because the nomenclature remains the same. The sky is still the sky, even if the descriptors change; even if yesterday it seemed as if it was crashing down around us while today it is a beautiful haze that transports us to a higher place. And a tree remains a tree, even if yesterday it was menacing, reaching out to pull us down to hell, while today it is reassuring, embracing us in the constant beauty of nature.

I remain I, even if it doesn't always seem that way.

ONE DAY, I took a walk in the garden and it felt different. I rounded the corner and was confronted with a space that seemed entirely new. I noticed, for the first time, the way the lawn sloped down towards the ponds (had they even been there before?), the way the path went against the camber of the slope in a most pleasing manner and down towards a knot of trees with benches on each side, before making off towards the fields beyond.

I noticed that the other path, which hugged the side of the building and followed it around the corner, was lined with low evergreen bushes, interspersed with flowers that were a beautiful testament to the imagination and dedication of the gardener. A figure who I must have seen innumerable times when I gazed blankly out of the window and into the deep maelstrom that lay perpetually before my eyes. Yet I had never registered him, let alone congratulated him on his facility with hoe and trowel.

I was so struck by this pleasing vision that I stopped in my tracks and stared. I had not seen any of this before; I had not noticed it. If someone had asked me, I would have been unable to describe the garden and would have seriously doubted if it was there at all.

While it would be tempting to suggest the garden had indeed not existed and had been constructed since my last walk just to perturb me (which is a thought process I might have entertained during the first few weeks after my arrival, before I saw the clarity in the light), I had to admit the change was within me. I was different. I don't know if it was the result of many imperceptible changes that accrued over time or whether it happened in one fell swoop, but that there had been a change was undeniable.

I headed over towards the knot of trees and sat down on one of the benches that looked out over the ponds. I watched the water, which rippled under a slight breeze, and placed my hands on the wooden seat. The knotted and varnished surface was alive to my touch, and I breathed deeply the clean air, which was lightly perfumed by nearby blossoms. It must have been late spring.

I HOPE this isn't all sounding pretentious. I'm trying to get across the idea everything seemed different but it wasn't; rather, it was me who was now alive to my surroundings. Thinking about it, the last time I can recall before then of having been aware of the texture of a park bench or the bark of a tree or the smell of flowers in the air must have been when I was a teenager, before I left home and went to university.

. . .

I HAVE A THEORY. About the exit from the Garden of Eden.

It is an entertaining story, of course. But if we assume it is not historical record, but rather an allegory designed to offer the first important moral lesson of the Old Testament, I think we can observe something rather interesting about the human condition.

Eve eats from the tree of knowledge of good and evil. No matter how she was encouraged to do so, she did, and in doing so went against the advice of God. This leads to the fall of man, Adam and Eve becoming aware of their nakedness, and their eventual expulsion from the Garden of Eden.

For those who do not think of that story as historical record, the question then becomes: — What does it mean? What is it intended to indicate? It must have a meaning, otherwise it would not have been included in the Old Testament in the first place, and not given such importance in the teachings of Christianity. Indeed, even if one does believe it is historical fact, why include that story about the life of Adam and Eve over any another?

There have been many interpretations of what this story can mean. Many of the modern ones rather ham-fistedly try to apply a mishmash of Freudian and Jungian psychoanalysis to a story that was written at a time when that kind of structure for interpreting the thoughts and motivations of humans was not only a long way from being created, but would have been regarded as sacrilegious.

If we talk purely about the Christian world, the stories in the Old Testament were recorded and distributed by monks and other members of the faithful. They were guarded by the priests and bishops for recounting orally during masses and other moments of spiritual instruction, or visually via illustrations and paintings. They were intended to offer a moral guide to people in their day-to-day lives.

It goes without saying the vast majority of the intended

audience for these stories were illiterate. That is not to denigrate them as people but to point out that, if the stories were to be transmitted only orally or pictorially, there were a limited number of messages that could be included. Complex analyses of the relationship between the id, ego and superego were not the order of the day, just as they would not be now, no matter that any interpretation can be applied to a story after it has been created.

For me, the Old Testament in general is a Judeo-Christian interpretation of how humanity arrived at the point it found itself when Christ was born. The opening chapters of Genesis are about the creation of the world, and I believe the story of Adam and Eve is about the origins of humanity. Not humans themselves but the human condition.

The eating of the fruit of the tree of knowledge of good and evil; the fall of man; Adam and Eve becoming aware of their nakedness and their eventual expulsion from the Garden of Eden... this is to me all an allegory of the transition from childhood to adulthood; of the descent from innocence and emotional and sexual immaturity to becoming aware of our nakedness and its potential. It is also the story of becoming aware of the true intentions of people and starting to see the world as it really is, in all its messy and contradictory complexity; a place where we have to do battle with ourselves and other people simply to remain true to our beliefs.

Moving from the state of childhood innocence to an adult understanding of the complexities of life is enriching, but in many ways disappointing. We spend our childhood wanting to grow up, but we realise once we get there the destination is not as edifying or satisfying as we had presumed, and the supposed joy of achieving glory and fame is grubby and brutal when viewed up close.

This is the disappointment Adam and Eve felt, and God

too, in witnessing their loss of innocence. They became greater, wiser people, but their time in the Garden of Eden was, by definition, over. And when we experience this as we pass through puberty, we spend the rest of our lives searching for the shadow of that innocent place.

As I sat on the bench and looked out over the ponds, I wondered what to do next. And as simple as that sounds, it was perhaps one of the most significant thoughts I had had in a long while.

For longer than I could remember, I had dwelt almost exclusively in the past, with only occasional forays into the present for purely practical purposes: hunger, in all its senses, and sleep. Terrible sleep. The rest was a constant swirl around the maelstrom of what had happened to me in the past, and why.

I had been trapped, unable to see even a glimmer of a way out. Yet there I was, sitting on a bench in a garden, over-looking the ponds and wondering what to do next.

In other words, I had a future. I could see that now. For the first time, I was relieved I had spent so much time away from my daily life. I could see why I had needed to stay in that place. I had been tired, very tired. I'd let life get to me. I'd lost perspective and started to become paranoid.

I could see that now.

The next time we had a chat, *they* said I was doing well, and maybe we could start thinking about getting back to normal life, if I felt up to it. I confessed I was a little nervous, but I wanted my independence back, and to get home and be amongst my things.

The way they responded made me realise it was the most

135

sensible thing I'd said since I had been there. I thought back to some of our earlier discussions, when I told them what I thought about the world, and I have to confess I cringed. I must have shown that because they asked me what was wrong and I said I found it hard to believe the state I was in when I'd arrived. They said something like it is the journey you make and where you end up that is important, not your starting point.

I wanted to be cynical, as I was a little ashamed at my former self and wanted to lash out at them, but I decided it was rather a nice thing to say and meant to be encouraging. If they had wanted to make me feel bad, they could have done.

A week later, they told me they had been in touch with my company and my boss had agreed to take me back. Apparently, he had assumed straight away I'd needed to take a break due to exhaustion, and told them it was all completely understandable.

— He said: 'You don't even want to know how many cities we had sent him in 100 days. No wonder he needed a break from it all.'

Hearing that made me emotional. I had long accepted I would never be able to get back to my old life; I was irretrievably humiliated and no one would want to touch me, especially for a senior position in an international company. My fear had been, even if I could get myself straight again, I would be considered unemployable and end up as just another statistic. For the company to be willing to take me back was almost too much to ask.

Yes, there would be questions. Yes, people would talk behind my back, which would be excruciating. Yes, I would have to accept I would not be trusted in the same way as before. It was too late to change that now. But maybe, with a little renegotiation of my working life, I could perhaps end up better than before.

No, not maybe. I knew I could.

AND THEN ONE DAY, I was sitting on my bed when someone popped their head around the door and asked if I was ready. I could have said I'd been ready and sitting there for hours, that I'd been waiting for this moment for longer than I could remember.

I could also have said, after all I had been through, I would never truly be ready, that I was deeply afraid to even walk out of my room and wanted someone to come along and tell me it had all been a mistake and going back out there was a ridiculous idea. I could have said I would only know I was ready to go once I was out there, living my life in the moment and not thinking about this place.

But I merely said yes, stood, took one last look around my room and, trying to quell the fear that swirled within me, picked up my bag and followed him down the corridor.

I smiled as I followed him. I could see the light, so clear and bright, streaming in through the narrow windows lining the top of the wall and bouncing off the polished vinyl floor. My steps were light. I was light, and when I stepped outside, the sunshine warmed my soul.

One of *them*—someone who in other circumstances, at another time, I might have considered a friend—walked me down the path, chatting to me, asking me the simple questions we ask anyone who we know is nervous so we can fill the time, reinforcing a connection forged in difficult circumstances. I have to say I enjoyed our conversation, despite the nervousness. I enjoyed the normality of it.

We rounded the corner to the gate and I didn't notice at first, but then the sky crashed in as darkness flooded out of the ground and filled my soul. My knees gave way and my blood ran cold. My another-time friend saw and stopped, staring at me. I didn't want him to see what was happening to me, but I couldn't help it.

Waiting on the other side of the gate was Juliet.

SEVENTEEN

I SAID THE SKY CRASHED IN. MAYBE THAT'S NOT ENTIRELY accurate. It was more as if the walls I had built up around myself over the past few weeks and months fell in on me and everything they had been holding back, all the fears and memories and pain, came flooding in. I had thought all that was gone for good, that those things were dealt with and there was nothing more to say. That I was safe from myself and my past.

And yet there she stood, on the other side of the gate. She was smaller than I remembered, but just as present, leaning on one hip and shielding her eyes from the light.

Her hard eyes, which had stared at me so intently that night in the square outside the opera house. The rain on my skin, the cold reflections from the pavements, the echo of the traffic and the weight of the city; it all came back to me.

It was sunny, hot even, when I stood on the drive down to the gate, as my legs gave way, but I was wet, shivering in the night air as the cold penetrated my clothes and her words chilled me to the core.

My another-time friend was asking me something. Something about whether everything was okay. I turned to him, unsure what to say or do, unsure what to say about this woman who was waiting for me outside the gate.

— It's nothing. I'm okay.

He frowned at me, looking concerned.

— Your sister volunteered to take you home. She insisted.

— What? What did you say?

— She's been calling here every week since you got here to ask how you are. She told us not to tell you because she knows how sensitive you are about people knowing about your life, especially something like this. She said she didn't want to get in the way of your recovery.

— Oh, I see. How kind.

I stared down the drive to the woman waiting on the other side of the gate. She was no longer leaning on her hip and shielding her eyes, but standing up straight, feet slightly apart, staring intently, as if she was trying to understand what was going on.

— Your sister is the one who convinced us in the end we could let you go.

I stared at my another-time friend in amazement. He smiled.

— We like to make sure people have somewhere they can go, and someone they can rely on for support and help. You lead such a solitary life, Thomas. We weren't sure whether you could be left to your own devices and carry on the great work you've been doing here. It was very reassuring to us you would have such a close family member to hand, even if she hasn't come up in our discussions.

— I see. Of course.

What did all this mean? For a moment, I wondered whether I really did have a sister, one my parents had never talked about, perhaps given up for adoption, or they thought had died in an accident, but had, in fact, survived.

It didn't sound likely, knowing my parents to the little extent I did. They were so uniformly dull I couldn't imagine them hiding anything, let alone carrying around a secret so important, so dreadful as I had a sister they didn't want me to know about.

That's not fair. My parents weren't dull. They just weren't my kind of people. Not when they were together. After they separated, I got to know my father, more so just before he died, and he turned out to be a far deeper and more imaginative man than I could have ever thought beforehand. My mother flowered too once she was alone, but I had never known my father before, not even slightly.

— Do you want to see her?

I turned and stared at my another-time friend, surprised to find he was still there.

— Your sister. Are you happy to see her? If you'd prefer not, we can tell her you aren't ready and we can go back inside. No problem at all.

He gestured with his hand back up the drive to the main building. I had felt safe there. I was safe there. I thought about the bench and the view over the ponds. I thought about the common room, with its clarity and light, and I thought about having waited for this moment, to be led away from there, ever since I got there.

I could go back in. There would be no shame in that. Well, it would only be an extension of the shame I had already experienced by having gone there in the first place. And who would blame me for saying I am not ready? Who could say it wasn't a reasonable response to the situation, not to mention the appearance of my sister?

You don't have a sister.

I don't know who said that. I mean, I don't know which

version of me said that. It could have been any one of a number who seem to have a better handle on things than me.

You don't have a sister.

With some effort, I dragged myself out from that unreal part of myself and tried to remain in the present. I don't have a sister, I reminded myself.

So that means the small woman standing on the other side of the gate is who I think she is. It is Juliet.

I stared at her and squinted my eyes. Yes, it was her.

I know I should have questioned myself as to why she was there, what she wanted, why she'd come for me, how she'd found me, whether that meant all she had said to me was true. But I didn't care about all that. Not then.

— Yes, yes, of course I'm happy to see her. It's just a shock, that's all. I wasn't expecting to see her. I don't know when I would have met her. It's been quite some time, to be honest, even before I came here.

My another-time friend nodded understandingly.

— I'm sure you've noticed this, but I'm quite a reserved, private person, and I prefer to deal with things on my own. Maybe that's why I ended up here in the first place. Maybe if I'd found it easier to share my problems and issues, then I wouldn't have let them get so bad. So to have to confront the reality of other people knowing what I've been through so soon after it all happened, the day I get to rejoin society, with no time to organise the narrative into a form that is a little easier for me to present, is quite difficult.

I'M NOT sure I really said it like that. I don't think many people talk like that in real life, and it's certainly not how I would ordinarily say things. Even if I did say it like that, it sounds a little rehearsed, doesn't it? It sounds like I'm repeating what other people have said to me. Or maybe it's something I read in a book. It's the kind of thing I'd like to have had the presence of mind and clarity to say, however.

Correction: I did say something *like* that, but that is how I would like to have said it. If, that is, I'd had time to think about organising the narrative in a way that is a little easier for me to present.

Like now, for instance.

Whatever I said, the impression I wanted to get across was got across, and my another-time friend smiled, a little sadly I thought, and nodded, adding at least one 'of course' for good measure.

AFTER A COUPLE MORE SMALL PLEASANTRIES, we continued down the drive. My another-time friend accompanied me far enough to get a good look at Juliet and to give her a 'we've finally met after all this time talking on the phone' wave. He shook my hand, wished me luck and bade me farewell. Before I could properly respond, he turned away and walked back up the drive, disappearing from view.

I hesitated, hovering just in front of the gate, still entertaining slight thoughts of running back to the building and hiding away from everything. But eventually, I passed through the gate, trying not to look at Juliet, and thanked the porter.

On the other side, the light was different. It was harder and less warming. The breeze had a slight chill and I felt bare and unprotected in the light shirt and summer trousers I had been wearing when I arrived.

We stood staring at each other.

— So you believe what I told you, then?

— Why do you say that?

She stared at me hard, her cold, dark eyes trapping me and holding me in her gaze.

— You lied for me.

— Maybe I lied simply so I could get out of here.

She smiled knowingly and turned away from me, staring into my eyes until the last perfect curl of her dark hair obscured her view. Then she walked away, towards the only car in the visitors' carpark.

I stood and watched her and saw my only real chance of escape was already behind me. Of course, I wondered whether I could walk into the city from there, or find a bus, or beg them to take me back inside, banging on the gate until they opened up.

But I knew I wouldn't do any of those things.

She sauntered, which is the word the majority of people would use, to her car, fully confident she knew I knew I had no choice but to follow.

Or something like that.

After a moment, I trudged along behind her, knowing deep inside I didn't want it any other way.

EIGHTEEN

WE, SHE AND I, ARE IN MY FLAT, MY APARTMENT, MY ABODE.
She seems larger, as if she doesn't fit. I am tired, like I have
just woken up. But then again, I was like that a lot after I left
the place with the common room filled with clarity and the
ponds by the trees.

I am struggling to work out what is going on. I cannot
remember how long she has been there. The light, the angle
of the shadows, the soft intensity of the sunbeams suggest it
is mid-morning.

When did she get here? How did she get in?

I am wearing a pair of boxer shorts and a t-shirt, as if I've
just got out of bed and grabbed the first thing I could find.
She is standing in the middle of the room, fully dressed. She
has shoes on, as if she's just arrived or is about to leave.

There she stands, in the middle of the room, small but
nevertheless larger than the space. She is frowning. She has
her hands on her hips and her feet slightly apart. Her hair
seems perfect, the perfect amount of each dark curl hanging
in front of her perfect porcelain skin. The curve of her

cheekbones, the curve of her smile, the curve of her hard eyes, regarding me with such disdain.

She is a statue. An idol. A totem.

She is smiling sardonically, cruelly. She has said something that left me crushed and empty. Somehow, she has reached inside me and twisted my heart with her small, delicate hands. She has perfect hands, perfectly manicured with dark red nail varnish. Her sharp nails dig in and crush my insides until I cannot breathe.

I do not know or cannot remember what she said to me, but I know it was something so truly awful I may have blanked it from my mind to protect myself. Every time I approach the memory of what she must have said to me, my subconscious directs me elsewhere.

How did she find me? How did she end up inside my apartment?

I look around the room, searching for anything that could help me understand and stop her being so angry with me.

There is an empty coffee cup on the counter. It has been drunk from, by her. I can see traces of her dark red lipstick forming the bottom half of a perfect kiss on the side of the cup. The coffee machine is still on and there is coffee in the jug. But no other cup. Did I not have coffee? Maybe she drank mine.

Her shoes are by the door.

Wait.

I check again.

She is wearing shoes, and there is another pair of women's shoes by the door. My heart jumps and I become nervous. How long has she been here? Overnight? Days? Weeks? How long is it since I left the place? I thought it was only yesterday. I thought she picked me up from the place yesterday afternoon, drove me home and dropped me off.

I remember standing on the pavement outside my building, home but not home, disconnected from life, yet present within it, watching her drive away.

She had said nothing in the car. I turned to her to say something from time to time, but the words got stuck in my throat. Outside, in the air, before we got into the car, I had been fairly confident, but in the airless confines of the car, driving through the countryside and then the outskirts of the city, I was timid.

I couldn't explain it. Every time I turned to say something, I caught the shine in her hard eyes as she stared at the road ahead and I froze. Instead, I inspected the perfect curve of her cheekbones, the lift and fall of her lips, the caress of her dark curls on her skin.

From time to time, she would need to look in my direction, when we were at a junction or another car passed close by, and she noticed I was looking at her. She would glance at me without reacting, giving me nothing other than the observation of the fact I was staring at her. As if she expected it.

I hadn't needed to tell her where I live. She knew. By heart, it would seem, as she drove without the need to consult a map, or me, to find the shortest route through the maze of the city to my front door.

And there I stood, having taken out my bag and slammed the door. I remember the clunk, the firm reassurance of fine manufacturing. I had not noticed beforehand what car she had been driving, but I saw now it was an old Saab. Not in perfect condition but worn to the point of charm.

I bent down to say something through the window. I

wasn't sure I wanted to thank her, but I wanted at least to acknowledge her taking me home. So I bent down and she waited until I was looking straight at her before she drove off without even glancing in my direction.

And I stood there on the pavement outside my building, watching her drive away. It was afternoon. That was obvious from the angle of the sunlight and the length of the shadows. I presume I turned and went inside and up to my apartment. I don't remember.

My TABLETS. I have to take my tablets. Where are they? I glance around the room. I can't see them. Maybe they are in the bathroom. Or in the bedroom. I turn to get out of the chair, a dining chair, and then I remember she is there.

What is she doing here, standing in the middle of the room? Her demeanour suggests she is angry. Her perfect brow furrowed into perfect lines, her dark eyes shining and her mouth, coated in perfect dark red lipstick, twisted in beautiful fury.

I lean my elbow on the dining room table, and lean my head on my hand. I am so tired. And yet I have the feeling I have slept for a week. What is wrong with me? I glance over to the door and see her shoes. How long have they been there? How long has she been here? How long is it since I left the place?

I thought it was only yesterday.

— Are you even listening to me?

— What?

— I said: 'Are you even listening to me?'

— Yes, of course. I'm listening.

— What did I just say?

I look down at her feet. She is wearing heels. Black. They clack on the wooden floor as she moves from foot to foot.

— I'm sorry, I don't know.

— I thought so. Look, you need to pull yourself together. We are in the middle of an emergency and I need you.

I stare at her blankly.

— Don't tell me you have forgotten that as well? What happened to you when you were in there? What on earth did they do to you?

I want to say they gave me clarity, but it all seems like such a long time ago, as if it all happened to someone else. Or was it just a dream? I want to reach into the clarity, to hold on to it, to keep it with me, but it is slipping away from me, drifting into the distance.

— Well?

Then it all comes back to me in a flood. The Japanese restaurant, Lucy, running out into the street to find her. The table at the pizza place, trying to talk to the waitress, her tattoos and the magnificent parrot with its black iridescent feathers and glass dark eyes, staring at me. The pain in the opera house when I saw my friend. The white dove and reaching out to touch her wing. The blank faces, the sheep in the lecture room and seeing *him* again outside the conference centre.

I look up at her, amazed.

— The androids, I say. — We have to stop the dark forces replacing all of humanity with androids.

— Finally. Where the hell have you been? There is no time to waste. We have to act now.

— I just need a bit of rest, to recuperate a little.

As I say this, my eyes begin to shut and sleep washes over me.

— This isn't a game. This is happening. Now. We're talking about the human race here. It's being replaced, one by one, and you want to have a rest?

— Who are you? I shout. — Really? I didn't ask you to

come into my life. I didn't want you to get me involved in all this. I would have simply got on with my life if it hadn't been for you.

Oh how we lie when we are cornered. Even then, right in that moment, I know what I am saying isn't true.

She stares at me. The sardonic smile returns. Her perfect hands resting on her perfect hips, with her feet slightly apart.

— How do I know you are who you say you are? I don't even know if Juliet is your real name.

Her eyes harden. — It isn't.

— W-what?

I stare back at her, afraid. Afraid of what is happening to me, afraid of this woman standing in my apartment. Is she even the same person who picked me up and dropped me outside the building?

— What is your name? I ask meekly.

She tilts her head and looks at me pityingly.

— Helen. Where did you get Juliet from? You've never called me that.

— It's what I call you all the time. Ever since we met. I've been calling you that ever since you came here to stay.

What? What did I just say? But I only got back yesterday. How can she…?

And then I see it. Her clothes in the wardrobe, the coat in the hall. The shoes by the door. I see it now. Waking up and her being there. Her coldly walking out of the room, without a word, and the perfection of her form glimpsed as she pulls a sheet around her. Her silence as we sit together in the morning, not knowing what to say to her.

But it all must be just a dream. I only got back yesterday.

What about my tablets? What happened to those? I look up and am surprised to find her standing there in front of me, with her hands on her hips.

— You've never called me Juliet, she repeats.

NINETEEN

I woke up. It was morning. A bright sunny day. I listened for a while, to nothing. The apartment seemed empty. A train rumbled by in the distance.

I ran my hands across the bed, kicked back the duvet and looked around the room.

I am home.

The wardrobe door was open and I could see my things hanging there. My clothes from last night were on the chair. There was my book on the bedside table. Beyond lay the living room, the bathroom, the kitchen.

I ran my hand across the bed and cried. I don't know exactly why. There seems to have been relief that I was back in my bed, lying there on a sunny day, almost able to imagine that nothing had happened. I was back at the time when I had just bought the apartment and was starting again after the divorce.

But I was so tired. Maybe that was why I cried. I was so tired I didn't know what to do with myself. I thought about getting up and doing something, but I didn't know what to do.

. . .

TWENTY MINUTES later I stumbled out of the bedroom and into the living room. My things were everywhere, strewn around. The place looked as if I had been having a party and hadn't bothered cleaning up. Either that or it had been ransacked by someone looking for something. I stared out of the window at the river and blinked, yawning as I adjusted my eyes to the bright sky and the reflections on the water.

Coffee. I need coffee.

I took a cup from the cupboard and yawned again as I debated whether I wanted an espresso or a filter.

Definitely an espresso.

While waiting for the machine to finish, I leaned against the counter, glancing around the room, checking all was as I remembered it.

HOME. What a tenuous concept that is, once you look hard enough. I had called this place, this flat, this apartment, home because it was where I kept my things and where I went to when I wasn't staying somewhere else. But how much time had I actually spent there? In the years since I had bought it, maybe only a couple of months in total, and then rarely more than a week at a time. Yes, I had been happy to buy a place and call it my own, but it seemed I didn't want to live there on my own. The reality was, I suppose, I had never really learned how to live on my own. I was afraid of it.

Actually, I was afraid of myself. I had kept myself moving, non-stop, ever since the divorce, just so that I wouldn't have to deal with myself. Just so I wouldn't have to examine myself up close. And I had come up with ever-more elaborate strategies over the years to achieve that, taking jobs and roles that took me further and further away from myself.

It was my excuse for never having a partner, for never having a dog, for never really having any friends, for never doing anything for myself or having a hobby. All I did was hop from place to place, always running, never standing still.

WHAT WAS it she said to me, that long-lost other her from long ago? The one who might have been the one I married if things had turned out differently? What did that other her say to me, all those years ago, when I first saw myself falling apart?

— I just want someone I can stand still with and I don't think you are capable of that.

Her words pierced me and slowly made their way through my consciousness like a worm, burrowing deeper and deeper inside me.

I am writing about this now, but as I think of it, she and I were standing by the river—the one I could see outside my window when I was living in my apartment, but not the river I can see now as I type these words.

It is late at night when she says that to me. Well, late-ish. Around midnight. I am sure it's been raining as the pavement is shining. But that could simply be a received idea, a trope, as they say in the film world.

Maybe it wasn't like that but let's go the whole hog and say the moonlight is shining on the rain-soaked pavements and we stand under a streetlamp, looking out over the heavy black river as it winds its way slowly, majestically, to the sea. (That's a metaphor for motion and travel, by the way, the darkness of the water indicating my fear and anxiety.) There are buildings on the other side of the river, which is obvious as otherwise it wouldn't be much of a city, and their twinkling lights reflect on the water, casting a shimmering, dancing light towards us. So far, so clichéd.

I am about to leave on a trip—the next morning sounds better than 'soon'—and she has to catch her last train home. We've had dinner, a lovely dinner made bittersweet by the knowledge soon we must part. And so we walk along the river. Let's say hand-in-hand, although I don't think we were, and we stop under a streetlamp and look out over the water. Rachmaninov's Piano Concerto No. 2 in C minor (you know, the famous one) plays in the background. I have on a suit and a trilby, and a raincoat with the collar turned up, and she has her hair set just-so and an anxious look in her eyes.

— I'd be a damn fool if I didn't kiss you right now.

No one says that to anyone, although I might have if I had been of a certain persuasion.

— Oh don't, Thomas. You can't say that because then I'd go and do something stupid like fall in love with you.

ALL VERY NOËL COWARD. But what really happened is I didn't know what to say because I was leaving and I didn't want to lose her, yet I knew I couldn't promise anything. That's assuming, of course, she would have been interested in anything I might promise.

We talked about this and that, I made some jokes, and then she fell quiet.

— I just want someone I can stand still with, and I don't think you can, or are capable of it, or whatever sounds best to you when you're trying to remember this moment several years later.

I added that bit at the end for effect. I remember exactly what she said, but it's between me and the long-lost other her from long ago.

· · ·

ALSO, I have to confess I lied earlier. Where I am sitting to write this, I cannot see a river. I said I could because it seemed neater, more poetic. What I can see from the desk where they keep the typewriter, and thus the place we are allowed to use it, is a line of trees. And when the wind blows through them and the branch undulate in waves it sometimes sounds like running water.

THAT MOMENT, those words the long-lost other her from long ago said to me have stayed with me. Sometimes, often, they come back to me. They remind me we can lose things if we do not see them for what they are.

After that moment standing by the heavy black river, when I got back from the trip, I married the first woman I met. I think I was in grief. She, the long-lost other her from long ago who might have been the one, had moved on. She'd realised there is no point waiting around expecting people to do things of which they are not capable. And she didn't want to put her heart at risk for someone who did not know how to take care of his own.

So the moment passed, she moved on, I saw what I had missed, and I married the next woman I met.

Is all that tantamount to some kind of advice? If it is, don't listen to me.

I DRANK my coffee while leaning against the counter, staring out of the window of my apartment at the river beyond, the caffeine slowly bringing me to wakefulness. By the time I had finished the cup, I tingled with energy, and wondered what I should do.

That wasn't the first time I had thought that of late, but it was different the second time around. I had spent the previous few months unable to do anything for myself. I had been under constant watch and constant care. Simply to be able to go for a walk in the gardens had been something of enormous significance, but now I had the whole of the city before me. I could do anything, everything.

In addition to which, it was not long after I'd experienced the clarity of the light in the common room, with its huge windows or wall made of glass blocks, that I realised the coffee there was terrible. I brought the subject up several times, but *they* always avoided the issue, making bland comments about availability, cost or some other such nonsense, all of which I never quite believed. It was only later that it occurred to me they may have chosen that rank, bland, dark-brown industrial drink they had the cheek to call coffee because they didn't want us to get too excited.

So for me to lean here, in my own apartment, in complete silence, drinking an excellent cup of coffee (even if the grains were a little old), with no one to tell me what to do or what would be available to watch on the television tonight, or to go back to my room, or when I should take my tablets…

I froze.

My tablets. Where are my tablets?

I glanced around the room.

Where are they?

I thought back to when I'd arrived home.

Where had I put them? On the table? But they weren't there. In the bathroom? I went in, still carrying my coffee cup, and looked everywhere. Nothing.

I started to panic.

What have I done with them? Where are they?

I thought about having to go to my doctor and explain everything so I could have another prescription.

And then it hit me. When I had stumbled into the living room and found her standing there, she had been putting something into her bag. She'd turned around as if she'd been startled. Then she got angry and started an argument.

I looked down. There, on the edge of the white porcelain cup, were fine traces of dark red lipstick. My heart sank. I didn't want to think she had taken my tablets. What for? I needed them. And how long, exactly, had she been there in the apartment?

I remembered the second pair of shoes by the door and spun around. They were gone. She must have taken them with her. I sat down on the sofa, confused, unsure what to think.

And then the phone rang.

TWENTY

I STARED AT THE PHONE. THE NUMBER WAS WITHHELD, SO I should have had no idea who was calling. But I knew who it was.

I let it ring, increasingly nervous at the consequences both of picking up and not picking up.

Now she has rung me, I am trapped either way. Either I pick up, in which case I will have to deal with what she says, or I do not pick up, and then she knows I am avoiding her. Either way, she has one over on me.

IT WASN'T LIKE this when we didn't have mobile telephones, of course. If someone rang your house or desk, it was perfectly legitimate not to pick up. The person calling would assume they had simply missed you, or you were busy or temporarily indisposed, all of which was fine, unless they were of a suspicious nature. The phone itself stayed in one place while you moved about, so not responding did not imply anything other than a lack of proximity.

Now, however, one takes one's mobile telephone with one

wherever one goes, even to the toilet. That is the assumption, and is generally the case. Therefore to not pick up, to not respond, when someone telephones becomes an act in itself, an implied defiance against their call. You are either saying you do not have the time to speak to them, therefore indicating the caller is of a secondary priority, or you haven't got your telephone with you, implying any caller is of a secondary priority.

Of course we may not always be able to respond. As I said, we could be in the toilet, where taking a call, especially in a work or public convenience, would be deemed inappropriate. Or maybe we are in the shower.

You could simply not take your mobile telephone with you when you go out, but that would leave you open to accusations of being the kind of idiot who doesn't know what a mobile telephone is for, having missed the clue in the name. Or maybe you have it switched off, in which case you would fall into a slightly different version of the same category of individual.

Now, sitting here, typing this, watching the river of air flow through the trees outside the window, I confess I no longer have a mobile telephone. We are not, officially, allowed to have them in here, or we weren't until there was a change in the regulations, and there seemed little point in keeping it if I was unable to use it.

Anyway, who would call me now?

To be honest with you, I don't miss it. I can still call people if I wish via the payphone, but to have been removed from under the weight of always being reachable, and now being able to choose when I connect to the outside world, is something of a pleasure. More than that, it's a relief.

I suppose that's why they initially told us we couldn't have them. Ubiquity has forced them to change their stance, however. The notion of course being, because something ubiquitous, it is essential, as demonstrated by it being everywhere. That is not a logical assumption, however, as that which is essential is not always ubiquitous and not all that is ubiquitous is essential.

I ALWAYS KNEW, somewhere in my mind, that no longer having a mobile phone would be a relief, but I became aware of it fully when I came here. Privation, separation, isolation (after a fashion) are as liberating as they are restricting.

My grandfather said, in a manner of speaking, true freedom is to follow the rules, as only then will you be left alone. It sounds counterintuitive. And it's a mantra for conformism, if read that way. However, if you look at it another way, as long as you follow the rules, by which he meant general social conventions, then the rest of you is free to do as you please, the only limit being your imagination. And it is by placing limits on ourselves we truly learn to innovate and invent, and thus explore new spaces and ideas.

And that is freedom.

Take a spacecraft. By following the rules of physics and learning to use them to our advantage, we have extended our reach into the infinite.

It sounds good, doesn't it, when I put it like that. But it doesn't seem like that when they take your mobile telephone away without asking.

I STOOD there in the kitchen, hesitant, nervously staring at the vibrating ringing telephone as it danced on the surface of the counter. I knew then I was anything but free.

And then it stopped. The screen went blank and I stared at it for a second before looking out of the widow at the river beyond. Although it had been sunny before, the sky was now filled with clouds, turning the water a dirty grey and bringing a chill in the breeze that whipped across the surface of the river.

Actually, that's not true. It was still blazing sunshine, and the reflections of the sunlight danced across the tops of the waves. I said that about the cloud and the drop in temperature because that was what had happened to me. I had become shadowed, cold and dark, but I preferred to use a visual cliché.

And there it was again, the phone jumping into life. Still no caller ID, but I knew, just as I had known the second I saw her waiting outside the gate, she would never leave me alone until she had got what she wanted from me.

When I stopped having a mobile phone, when they took it away from me, I wondered what would happen when someone tried to phone me. I had told no one I'd been taken here, not even what was left of my closest friends.

I had no family, no one to care about me, no roots. If someone called, would the line go dead and then they would wonder if I am also dead? Or would my number be reassigned and they would get someone else entirely, someone unaware of me and my existence, causing embarrassed confusion until the facts had been established?

And what facts would they be? That I no longer had this number? The caller would still be none the wiser as to why.

Then I thought about the calls I had received on my mobile telephone in, say, the year before I was brought here. Discounting the insurance sales calls and the suggestions I had recently been in a car accident and might I like to pursue a claim, I had received no personal calls at all. Some texts, yes, but not a single phone call.

Apart from when she called me.

THE PHONE DANCED on the counter and a creeping nausea rose up through me. I let it ring off and continued staring at it. Outside, the sky turned grey, cracked and fell in, churning the river into a maelstrom of fear and despair.

But I didn't need to look out of the window to see that.

The phone rang again and I picked it up and stared at the door, as if she would burst in at any moment.

The other end of the line was silent.

I thought for a moment I was mistaken, that a computerised voice would talk to me about a fictitious car accident. But her cold, hard breath was there, seeping out of the phone and penetrating my soul.

— W-what do you want? My voice was brittle and shaking.

Silence.

— Hello?

— You know what I want.

She spoke slowly, pushing her words into me.

— I don't know. I don't know what you want.

— Yes, you do. You have always known. Meet me at the café in twenty minutes.

— What café?

— You know which café.

— How? How do you…

— Bring money.

— What? Why?

— You'll need it.

Before I could say anything else, she rang off.

I stared at the window and the bright sunshine dancing

on the waves that scuttled across the river. My attention was momentarily caught by a passenger ferry, and I was hauled back into the present.

Money? Surely I must have misheard. But no, I knew what she said.

She didn't even say how much, or why.

— You are such an idiot. After all that, to demand money? Is that all she wanted in the end?

But what if I'm wrong about her? I don't know the full story, of course. Maybe there's a legitimate reason why she wants money and she can't say it over the phone. Don't forget this is serious. Dark forces are taking over the world, replacing humanity one by one with androids. Maybe your phone is being tapped and she dare not explain.

I glanced around the room, startled for a moment, wondering if someone was there. I thought I saw a shadow and went out on to the balcony to check. There was no one. It was hot. A warm breeze was blowing up from the river. The world seemed so much calmer and more reasonable from out there.

Why don't I spend more time on the balcony? It's nice.

Concentrate, you fool. What can this all be about?

I stared at the patio door, wondering what would happen if someone locked me out.

Maybe I am locked out.

I pulled the door open and, relieved, went back into the apartment.

What shall I do? What should I do?

I contemplated meeting her in twenty minutes but I didn't want to go.

— You don't have to go.

I turned around and jumped in shock.

There, in the middle of the room, was the magnificent parrot, standing right next to me. Her glass dark eyes, surrounded by iridescent black feathers, stared into me. Her feathers rustled as she moved slightly then shook her head, all the while staring at me.

I turned away. I had to.

Out of the corner of my eye, I saw the magnificent dove disappearing into the bedroom. I ran after her but there was no one there.

— Where are you?

I didn't recognise my own voice. My phone was in my hand. How did it get there? The café. How did she know about it? Twenty minutes. But when did she call? I checked my phone. Only five minutes ago. And it takes five minutes to walk there. I have time.

I can't go. She only wants me for my money.

But what if the money is to fight the dark forces?

I wondered if my phone was tapped. Turning, I saw another shadow. I ran towards the balcony but stopped myself in my tracks, worried I'd get trapped out there. I went back into the bedroom and stared at the white duvet.

The magnificent dove. I was sure she was in here, just a second ago. But maybe the reason I couldn't see her now was she was lost in the white sheets.

If you look carefully, you can see her, underneath, waiting.

Maybe if I get in to bed, everything will be okay.

I pulled back the duvet. There was nothing there. I lay down and pulled the duvet over my head. I closed my eyes and the magnificent dove appeared under the duvet, her shimmering white feathers rustling as she approached me. She kissed me, her white beak surprisingly soft and tender. Then she was the magnificent parrot, pulling me into her, into her iridescent black feathers, and I was suffocating.

Then she was Juliet or Helen and I threw back the duvet, panting for breath in the empty room.

TWENTY-ONE

WHEN I GOT TO THE CAFÉ, I COULDN'T SEE HER. I HAD secretly hoped, of course, she wouldn't come. Maybe she'd had a change of heart. Maybe I'd missed her. I checked my phone. I was only five minutes late.

I hesitated outside the café, glancing furtively inside to see if she was there.

Maybe she's at a corner table out of sight. I should go inside and look properly. Otherwise what's the point in coming at all?

What indeed?

I glanced again and caught the eye of the waiter I talked to, and regretted not having looked away sooner. He smiled and beckoned me in. Of course, he asked me how I was. Of course, he asked me where I'd been. He mentioned I looked younger, I'd grown a beard. He even said I looked happier.

But he clearly could not see what I saw reflected in his eyes. I saw I was empty. I had lost my presence, my sense of self. I seemed smaller somehow, less engaged, my attention caught by every sound. I was nervous, edgy, with fleeting glances taking my eyes away from him, away from the moment. My hair was less lustrous, the whites of my eyes a little grey, my tongue a little slow in my mouth.

He didn't mention any of those things. He tried his best to hide his surprise and make me comfortable, as if the only changes he could see were for the better.

I remarked on how well he looked and how I'd missed his Chai Latte. He smiled as if he was relieved and got me a drink on the house. I watched him from outside myself and it occurred to me I had underestimated our previous interactions. I had missed something important. We did have a connection, and I was too lost in my own maelstrom to be able to see it.

He handed me my Chai Latte, just how I like it, he said, and patted my shoulder and told me to come back again soon. I told him I was looking for a friend who was not there and had to go. In doing so, I cut short a moment of fraternal intimacy. Tears came to my eyes, which I tried to hide by laughing and turning away. I promised in a breaking voice I would be back soon.

Then I walked out of the café, having forgotten entirely why I was there.

Until I saw her standing outside, right in front of me as I navigated my way through the tables strewn across the pavement.

She stood there with her arms folded and a sardonic grin on her face. Her perfect mouth, painted in dark red, twisted into amused cruelty. It was a tug on the hook in my lip, dragging me back to the dark place where the only emotion was fear.

— Are you ready?

I stopped abruptly and stared at her, captivated by the perfect curls of her perfect black hair hanging down over her dark shining eyes and porcelain skin.

A statue. An idol. A totem.

· · ·

DO YOU MIND? You, the reader. I'm talking to you, whoever you are; that is, if you are not that other self to whom I am addressing all this. (He doesn't mind. He never does.)

Do you mind? That I keep doing that? You know, switching from past tense to present tense and back again? And switching from the events to me to addressing you about how writing this is affecting me?

I'm not doing it on purpose. It's not a conceit. I don't really know what that means, in any case. I'm not a writer, after all.

When I am writing, eyes flicking between typewriter keyboard and typed page, checking the one then the other, while trying to type at the same speed as I am thinking... that is already quite enough for me to be dealing with, let alone thinking too much about *how* I'm writing.

I mention it because I noticed I was doing it the other day, when I was trying to find something I had written so I could talk about it with *them*. I saw I jump from the past to the present and back again, and from telling the story to addressing you, and then back again.

Do you mind? I think I do it when I get so involved in recalling a moment that I can no longer separate the me in the moment now from the me in the moment then, and it becomes the present, just as I lived it. After a while, I settle back down again, regain a little distance and perspective, and I switch back to the past tense.

It's not what is called a literary device. It's just me. It's the same when I address you directly. It's how I talk in real life. Although I admit sometimes I do it because I am nervous about writing the next part. I'm afraid to dredge up the memories. But they keep telling me it's a good exercise.

I hope you don't mind.

.   .   .

— READY FOR WHAT?

— You know what. To leave. Are you ready to leave? Now.

— Leave where?

She clenched and unclenched her jaw and sighed. She looked down at the pavement, then at the tables ranged along the pavement behind me, then down the road towards whatever you would like to imagine was on the high street. All the while, I was filled with the most delicious dread, the most intoxicating fear.

What is happening to me?

I didn't know what to say. She was forceful, angry. And I was afraid. Afraid I had displeased her. But I was afraid of something else, too; something I couldn't name, or didn't want to.

Abruptly, she walked down the road, away from the high street. I watched her for a second, noticing for the first time she was wearing high-heeled leather boots, which is why she must have seemed so much taller and more present than before.

I considered walking away, going home and forgetting about this whole thing. But I knew that wouldn't be possible, even to entertain the idea was ludicrous. I would like to think I considered walking away and rejected the idea, as that would lend me some degree of autonomy and personal agency, but I had known even before I got to café I wouldn't be capable of doing that. I knew I would do whatever she told me to do.

Besides, she could get into my apartment, so there was clearly no escape from her.

.   .   .

I HURRIED AFTER HER. I remembered I had the Chai Latte in my hand and threw it in the nearest bin, and then ran to catch up with her.

— Please wait, I heard myself say.

She stopped and wheeled around. She was close to me, uncomfortably so, and she stared at me intensely. I looked around and saw we had stopped on a secluded part of the path, hidden on either side by trees and hedges, and there was no one around, all of which only heightened my fear and anxiety.

— Why are you here? she hissed at me.

— B-because... I don't know.

— Stop playing games. Why are you here?

I swallowed and looked up and down the path. I wished someone would come along to interrupt us, to give me a chance to collect myself.

— Look at me.

I turned and she trapped me there, in the dark infinity of her eyes.

— You answer me. Why are you here?

I wanted to say 'I don't know' again, but I knew I couldn't.

— Because I want answers, I said meekly. — And to stop the dark forces and save the human race.

I didn't know whether I believed that any more, but I knew that was what she wanted to hear. She smiled slightly.

— Then you need to come with me. And you need to do everything, and I mean everything, I say. You will obey me without question. Understood?

I swallowed and stared at her. Her eyes sparkled and she licked her perfect lips.

— Say it.

I swallowed again, aware I had become someone I did not know at all.

— Say it.

Her words penetrated deep inside me.

— I need to come with you.

— And?

— I need to do everything you say.

— And?

— I will obey you without question.

— Good.

I have no idea why I, this unknown version of me, was saying these things to this woman, out loud, and yet I understood in that moment I had waited all my life to say them to someone.

— But I don't even know your name, I stammered.

She smiled again, differently this time. Cryptically.

I was protesting by saying that, but it was merely a gesture, a last stand purely for ceremonial purposes, to remind myself I am not simply an automaton, a slave. And to remind her that, behind the passive acceptance of her control over me, there was an independent human being who was falling away from himself.

— But you already know my name.

— Helen?

She regarded me like a scientist inspecting a caged rat or a prison guard staring at a prostrate inmate. Dispassionately. That's the word. Almost cruelly. I the object, I the possession, I the nothing.

She turned and walked away and I followed, without hesitation, without considering any alternatives. But then, a break in the spell; a line thrown from what remained of my previous life, pulling me back.

— Wait.

She walked on.

— Wait, Helen.

She stopped and turned, and placed her hands on her hips.

— What is it?

— I need to know something.

— Well?

— What happened to my tablets? The ones they gave me to keep me stable.

— You don't need those any more.

She turned on her heel and walked on. A wave of emotion flooded up through me. I followed her, with tears in my eyes, wanting so desperately to leave, to have the strength to turn and walk away, but I knew I could not.

TWENTY-TWO

WE WERE IN THE CAR, THE TWO OF US, DRIVING THROUGH THE city. But it was no longer a place I recognised. I had not been away that long, but it had been quite some time since I truly lived there.

When I first arrived, I was young, not long out of university; excited and ready for the world, thinking I could take on the city and win. Whatever that means. I think I'd watched a lot of American movies from the forties and fifties around that time.

If I can make it there / I can make it anywhere

That's what happens when you grow up in a place where it rains a lot. You watch a lot of Gene Kelly movies. You know the one where he's a sailor and goes to New York? They showed it a few weeks ago. Here, in the common room. I couldn't bring myself to watch it.

. . .

I WANTED TO BE SOMEONE. Of course we are all 'someone', but I suppose the phrase means to be someone significant, successful, someone with meaning and a place in the world. We all have a place in the world. It's just that unless it comes with a little fame, as in other people know about your place in the world enough to be able to talk about it, then you are considered a 'nobody'.

It's all a little vacuous, when you think about it. Am I not somebody, even now? Will I become somebody by writing these words and setting down my story? Perhaps not unless other people read what I have written. And even then, I will not be aware of any fame, of having become somebody.

We all have a place in the world, in our local community, whatever and wherever that may be. My place in the world used to be a little wider than it is now, both geographically and in terms of the number of people I knew. But I am known better, more deeply in here than I have been anywhere else in my life.

Before, I was relatively well known in a small world, a well-regarded specialist in my field, enough to be asked to give lectures and mentor younger people who would like also to become specialists. But everything that was known of me was a combination of my projected image and their projected assumptions.

Who I was, as a person, mattered not. Indeed, it was undesirable that I should pull back the veil and reveal the human. Perhaps it was permissible from time to time, but only a little, just to remind everyone I was human.

WHAT IS it to be known?

When I was on the conference centre steps, unable to get back in, having seen my friend who is dead, and when I called out to the session chair... This was the man who had introduced me to the audience and with whom I had conversed on several occasions, next to whom I had sat for the odd social dinner.

This was a man I knew well enough to know he had a wife (name forgotten), children (numbering between two and three, aged between six and eleven years) and had grown up in Oslo or Stockholm. He had lived in America on the east or west coast for several years while teaching at a local university.

Is that what constitutes knowing someone? Is that what it means? And is that how he knew me? A few half-remembered facts and a vague sense of my personality? Was he a friend? Perhaps, although not enough to come to my aid when I was stranded outside the conference centre.

He'd always seemed so affable, if a little reserved. Every time I made a joke that presented a vision of the world that was anything other than concordant with propriety (by which I mean, every time I made a dirty joke), he ignored me. He preferred me not to make jokes at all, as far as I understood, but if I was to test his patience by attempting some sort of humour, I should at least keep it clean.

I read all this in the tense flicker of his eyebrows and the instant glazing over of his eyes whenever I misspoke.

I knew this man, I would have been able to spot him anywhere. I would always say hello, and he to me, and I would always have the sense when I saw him that, yes, here is someone with whom I can spend some time.

But he was not a friend. He was an acquaintance, and one who had no desire to take our friendship any further. I knew a lot of people that way. For example, I didn't really *know* anyone at work; I had made the mistake of being too familiar with someone in a previous job and was wary of repeating the error. My colleagues invited me out for drinks, of course, and of course I went from time to time, but I learned to be always at least one quarter distant, slightly non-committal.

I suppose it was prudent to be that way with my team, and my manager too. He treated me the same way as my maths teacher had done at school. I imagine it is how a kindly uncle might be: chummy, but with a protective arm around the shoulders, knowing that young Thomas wasn't quite ready for the big wide world, that he could get hurt out there.

Perhaps it was true. Perhaps I did need a protective uncle. But I didn't want them to see it that way.

I HAD AN UNCLE. He died when I was young. I think he was an alcoholic.

I HAD NO ONE. Not even those two friends I met up with after I saw Lucy in the Japanese restaurant. Not anymore.

I was alone, truly alone.

Yet I was only fully aware of it when I was in that car with her, perfect her, driving across a city I had once known a long, long time ago.

I really got to know the city when Lucy and I first worked together, and didn't we have so much fun. It was a golden time. Life was so fresh and new. Or maybe it was only to us.

We would go out after work several nights a week, trying bars, clubs, music venues and cheap dives. We met so many people and saw so many things. We made friends with people we would never have met had we not met each other. Lucy and I were the same age and had grown up in similar places, and now, finally, we were getting to live our dream of being with the people we read about in the magazines and saw on television.

The window on to another world had become our world.

AS WE DROVE across the city, perfect her and I, we went past a pub Lucy and I used to go to with her friends. Inside the car was only silence, yet a rowdy jumble of memories from that time crowded around in my head.

I smiled and turned to her. I wanted to tell her, to share my memories.

I was about to speak, but I saw the hard line of her jaw and her perfect lips, painted in dark red, pursed and tight. The curls of her perfect dark hair tumbled perfectly in front of her eyes, and I saw enough of her expression to know she was sparkling with determination and seriousness.

She swerved around a van and I was thrown around in my seat. She swore under her breath and I wanted to catch her words and pull them into me.

I don't know if it was because she was so obviously serious or because she made me feel like a lost child, but I regretted wanting to tell her about my memories of the pub, of its highly original decor, of the bands that would play on a Saturday night. It was stupid and inappropriate. I saw that now.

I was glad I hadn't said anything.

AT THE NEXT set of traffic lights, I gazed at her, taking her in.

She was aware I was looking at her. I could see her eyes involuntarily shoot a glance at me. I wanted to smile.

— How much money did you bring?

— What?

— How much money? How much have you got?

— I... I didn't bring any.

She turned and stared at me, her face incandescent with

rage. No, that's not quite right. No one's face is actually incandescent with rage. That happens to Elmer Fudd, or Daffy Duck. It's not even a very good cliché. It's empty as an idea.

No, she didn't look at me like that. I could have handled something so cartoonish. Instead, her eyes burned straight into my soul, and I shrank back into the seat, horrified at having made her so angry.

— Why not?

— I want... I want to know more about why...

— Get out.

— What?

— GET OUT OF THIS CAR, she shouted at the top of her voice.

I recoiled and, without thinking, opened the car door and scrambled out. I could see that the lights had changed and the cars in front were beginning to pull away. I hesitated and looked down at her, hoping she would change her mind. But I knew that was impossible.

Without looking up at me, she leaned over and pulled the door shut before putting her foot down and speeding away. I watched her car disappear into the distance before being lost in the endless circulation of vehicles.

I carried on watching for a while, half imagining she might come back and pick me up. I don't know how long I stood there at the junction, watching all the cars, trying to remember what hers looked like.

After a few minutes or maybe a few hours, I turned away and walked back the way we had come. It was surely too far to walk to my apartment, but I knew I would come across a bus or taxi eventually.

— Or maybe you could just walk home, a quiet, sensible version of myself suggested.

Maybe that is the me I am writing all this for.

177

— It might do you good, he said. — It might help to clear your head.

But as I trudged along the road, I saw, with a sinking heart, I was alone again, and a long way from anything like home.

TWENTY-THREE

THE NEXT MORNING, I LAY AWAKE IN MY BED, WONDERING WHO I was. I had drifted so far away from the person I knew, I did not recognise myself.

That is supposed to be a figure of speech. Shorthand for something much more complex.

I looked in the mirror and I no longer recognised myself.

How many times has that been said in books, in films, even in songs? I suspect it remains such a go-to for a certain type of emotion because it is meant to be jarring, as we normally look into a mirror to find ourselves, to reassure ourselves we are still there. And yet he (and isn't it always a he, a grizzled he, beaten by life) has looked in the mirror and seen a version of himself he does not recognise, and he doesn't know how to get back to his real self.

(By the law of averages, this must happen to women at the same frequency as it does to men, if it happens at all, but a breakdown in a woman is not lionised in the same way it is in men. In a man, a breakdown is portrayed as a heroic fight against one's demons. In a woman it's derided, dismissed as poor self-control, a reduction, a disappointment. It hardly seems fair.)

In any case, the cliché is clearly founded in the idea we obviously still look the same (otherwise we'd be mutilated), but the horror is what lies inside us no longer fits what we see in the mirror. We have let a side of ourselves we don't like become dominant, and we no longer match up to the image we wish to project.

Does that sound about right?

NONE of that applied to me, not that morning. Not when I lay in bed and wondered, with horror, who I had become.

I no longer recognised myself. However, this was a literal statement. I had caught sight of myself the previous evening while walking alongside a glass and metal building in a redeveloped area of the city. It had been a dock, I think, in previous times.

I saw my reflection in passing. I glanced across, caught by a flash of movement that corresponded to my own, and stared at the fast-walking person in the glass. Shocked, I stopped and looked at this man I did not know, then walked on quickly, my head turned to one side so I would not be able to see myself, or whoever that was in the glass, again.

THE PAVEMENT WAS grey-yellow in the streetlights, and pockmarked with dropped chewing gum. There were bins and a bus stop, and cracks in the tarmac and feet passing by. I dared not look at those people. They would have seen the shame and horror on my face. They would have known.

Surely they did know.

But know what, exactly?

That I had become a broken, decayed, derelict shadow of a man I once was.

I stopped by a set of traffic lights and looked around. My head was pounding and I was dizzy, uncomfortable inside my skin. The lights and the people and the cars and buses and taxis. The echoing sounds and the fluttering pigeons and the neon lights and the reflecting windows and the footsteps. The buildings staring down at me and the laughter, clearly directed at me, against me, and the clinking of glasses. And the everything, everything, everything, crowding, jostling, pushing, tugging at me. I was overwhelmed and lost and enticed and delighted.

Here was somewhere I could swim out too far and drown.

I CROSSED THE ROAD, between the cars and buses and taxis, and headed straight for a pub with its doors thrown open and hundreds of people standing, sitting, leaning, lounging on and among benches strewn around the doors. There was live music, an Irish folk band, and chatter and laughter and the hubbub I hadn't known for such a long time. I had of late been too afraid to go out. But there I stood, not sure what to do or why I was there.

There is no why. There is only now.

So I walked into the pub and pushed through the crowd of shouting faces and sweating bodies and stood near the bar, on the opposite side from the band, where the people smiled and talked. Near the bar, hovering, not pushing closer, not moving further away.

I didn't know what to do. I wanted a drink but I couldn't bring myself to get one. I wanted to be part of the pub, but I was behind glass, in a room on my own, a thousand miles away, watching it all transmitted live from earth.

Someone offered for me to go to the bar ahead of them and I politely declined. They—it was a he. He asked me if I was on my own. I said yes. He asked me if he could get me a drink. He was buying a round for a group of people he gestured to on the other side of the bar (I pretended to know where he was pointing) and said that one more drink on the tab wouldn't make much difference.

I smiled and was about to say no, it's okay, when I remembered the man I had seen reflected in the window of the glass and metal building. I didn't want to think of his fast-paced walk, his gaunt features and sunken eyes, his fear and his suspicion.

So I said yes. I pretended I was a normal human being who just happened to be out on his own for a quiet drink in the busiest bar in town.

What did I want?

I said, — I'll have whatever you are having.

THINKING ABOUT IT NOW, I realise that was a strange thing to say. What do you think, reader version of me? Normally one knows what one wants. We only say something like I'll have what you're having on a date or when we are trying to ingratiate ourselves with someone. Maybe I was trying to do that (the latter; I knew I wasn't on a date).

It had been more than a year since anyone had bought me a drink, and I wasn't sure when last I had had a conversation with someone. Just a conversation. No reason, no ulterior motive, no hidden agenda, no checklist or form to fill out afterwards, no result expected.

I was out of practice. I didn't know how to behave in polite company any more. So I said I will have whatever you are having, and he gave me a pint of lager, cold with bubbles.

I don't really like that kind of beer, but I was no longer myself. I was another person, so it didn't matter.

I am still no longer myself.

TYPING that made me stop and look out of the window. The trees have a slightly breeze in them today. They are calm and silent as they sway. Or they seem that way from where I am sitting, behind glass and a thousand miles away.

IT OCCURS to me I have 'no longer been myself' for longer than I have been myself, or at least the version of me that I, and perhaps some other people, would define as 'myself'.

I have been a broken, decayed, derelict shadow of myself for so long now, I calculated I have spent more of my life in this state than in any other, including puberty and childhood. That suggests the version of me I consider the reference standard, the 'normal', the 'me' I would describe myself as to others, was no more than a passing phase.

When you think about it, that means the broken, decayed, derelict shadow of me is the 'normal', the reference standard, and what I am holding on to as 'me' is outdated wishful thinking.

I SIPPED on that first pint as I followed him across the crowded pub, which seemed less rowdy and intense now I was no longer alone, to his group of friends. He had persuaded me—cajoled me, I suppose—to come and join him.

— No, no, you don't want to be on your own, not on a night like this. If you'd really wanted to spend the evening in isolation, you'd have stayed home, and if you'd really wanted a quiet night in a local pub, there is no way you would have come here.

Or words to that effect.

That could have been him or my better, more worldly self saying that.

— No, come with me and meet my friends. They're very nice, and I'm sure they'll like you.

Or words to that effect.

I wanted to run away, as we got nearer and nearer to his group, me sipping my fizzy pint and sticking close to his back as he wended his way through the crowd. But I couldn't run away. Not without him noticing, and that would have been more embarrassing than staying.

When we got there, he told me who everyone was and I instantly forgot their names. Then he disappeared to get the next batch of drinks. When he turned his back, his friends were less welcoming than he had led me to believe and either looked away, or stared at me with mild contempt and then looked away.

No, I definitely wanted to run away, but I couldn't bring myself to be back out there on the streets, walking along the road like a stray dog, on my own, being a person I didn't recognise. So I tried not to panic. I smiled at no one in particular and listened to the band, and told myself every-thing would be okay once he got back.

In a strange way, I was even a little euphoric.

WHEN HE CAME BACK, the man who'd bought me a drink, he saw I had been shunned by his friends. So he talked only to me, and the rest of his group slowly drifted away, either home or to see other friends, one by one, until there were only the two of us left.

He wouldn't let me buy a drink, not one, and he got me

pint after pint until I became drunk. The band stopped playing and I went to the toilet, wondering while I was in there whether I could escape out of a side door or window. But he was looking out for me when I came out.

We had some more drinks and sat on stools by the bar. He told me about some sadness in his life, and I didn't know what to say. I think he wanted me to open up about my life, but there was a wall of granite holding back a flood I dared not release. I became confused and a little upset and he didn't push me any further.

I was drunk, so was he, and I was unsure who I was. Was I the stray dog I'd seen on the street, or another me?

I was going to ask him what he thought about that but then the barman called time and we talked outside, him swaying as he told me we don't have to feel alone in this life and there are always people who want to listen and help and be there for people, and he wouldn't ask me for my number, but he would give me his and I could call him whenever I wanted, and that meant day or night, but just don't feel alone because we could all be alone, flotsam adrift on the ocean, but there are invisible wires that connect us all and all it takes sometimes is to recognise that and connect those wires, and then we can all be there for one another, so you are never alone, okay?

He patted me on the chest when he said that. I nodded and nearly cried. I took the piece of paper with his name and number scribbled on it, and I folded it carefully and put it in my pocket.

I was so overwhelmed by him and who he was that I didn't know what to say. He must have seen all of that passing across my face as he simply smiled, shook my hand and repeated he was there if I ever needed it, day or night. And then he walked away, swaying and stumbling a little. I watched him, with a warm glow around me, until he turned a corner and disappeared.

And then I was cold.

I THOUGHT about all of that the following morning, as I lay in bed and stared at the light and the shadows moving across the walls.

After a few moments, I got up, dressed and left my apartment. I passed a bank and took out as much money as my card would allow. As I was putting away my wallet, I found the note the man had given me with his phone number on. I screwed it up and dropped it into a bin.

When I arrived at the café, the waiter was not there and I inspected the faces of all of the customers. I stood outside and looked up and down the pavement. I noticed a car slowing down and drawing to a stop in front of me. She leaned over and looked up at me out of the passenger window.

— Get in.

I got in and we drove away.

TWENTY-FOUR

THERE WE WERE, IN THE CAR. SHE AND I. AT FIRST, I DIDN'T want to look at her. I was annoyed with myself. I wished I could have been stronger. I wished I could have said no. But I knew I could not.

I dared not look at her. Although I tried surreptitious glances, I was afraid she would notice. But I so desperately wanted to look at her, to see the perfect curve of her porcelain face and her perfect hair hanging down, dark and mysterious.

She was staring straight ahead, not even trying to look at me, to see me, to show she cared, even just a little bit.

I thought she saw me glancing at her and so I stared fixedly out of the window. We were taking the same route out of the city as the day before, but I didn't recognise it any more. I had walked every step back the afternoon before, trudging along the road alone, head down, trying to see no one, trying not to be noticed. By the time I had reached the city centre, far past my apartment, I'd had no idea where I was going.

I had no idea where we were going then, either.

. . .

THE CAR. She stopped it at the same traffic lights where she'd ordered me out of the car the day before.

— Where are we going?

— How much money did you bring?

I stared at her, unsure what to say. She was still looking straight ahead. It was the first time since she told me to get in that she had acknowledged my presence.

This is not how I want to be acknowledged.

— Did you throw away my tablets? I need them.

She turned to me and bored into me with such cold, piercing eyes that I shrank back into my seat and looked down at the floor.

— How. Much. Money. Did. You. Bring?

I swallowed and tried to think of something good and calming, not the glass dark eyes of the magnificent parrot and her iridescent black feathers. I tried to walk down Danziger Straße towards Eberswalder Straße to meet my friends. I tried to let it fill my mind, but her eyes creeped out from the shadows by the arches and burned into me.

— Three thousand. It's all I can take out in a day.

She looked me up and down like a piece of meat. I could see that out of the corner of my eye, even as I continued staring at the floor. I could sense it with every fibre of my being.

— Then we will have to come back again tomorrow.

She put the car into gear and drove off. I was elated to have passed the test, but I knew I was slipping further and further out of control and into her power.

WE DROVE AND WE DROVE. I don't know how long for or really where we went. I know we left the city far behind and passed others on the way, but my mind was so frantic I couldn't concentrate or distinguish one sign post from the next.

She said nothing, and I knew she did not want me to speak. I wouldn't have known what to say in any case. Or rather, I wouldn't have known what to say first. I had a thousand questions I wanted to ask, although I was afraid of the answers.

And I was angry. At her. At me. At everything.

Yet I was too afraid to say anything.

— How much further do we have to go?

I tried very hard not to sound like a scared child when I said that, but I am not sure if I succeeded. She glanced at me out of the corner of her eye, and then went back to concentrating on the road. I think I saw a smirk on her lips.

— You got into the car, didn't you?

— I didn't have any choice.

— Are you sure? I didn't force you. I simply opened the door.

I sighed.

— And you took out money for me. And yet you brought nothing other than your wallet and the clothes on your back. You knew we were going on a long journey and it would be to join the fight against dark forces taking over the planet, killing human beings one by one, but you didn't prepare for it or even ask where we would be going, for what purpose or for how long. Don't you find that strange? Weren't you even a little curious? Didn't you think you might want to take something other than your wallet with you? What do you think you will be doing at the other end? Do you think this is some sort of holiday?

— You said...

— I said. I said. You are very lucky you are with me, Thomas. The world is about to end if we don't do something to stop it. We are about to engage in a war, in which we could all be killed, trying to save humanity, life as we know it, everything we have ever lived for, and you are going to give your all to help save it. Are you prepared for that? Body and mind?

— I think so.

— You are going to be a hero, a saviour. Your name, and the names of all those who fight with you, will go down in history. You will be talked about for centuries to come. You will no longer have to worry about whether your life has meaning. It will have the greatest meaning possible. I, you and all the rest of us will have saved the world from a dark force that threatens to destroy us all. How does that make you feel?

I smiled, and then quickly suppressed it. She glanced across in time to see the smile.

— That's right. You can be happy. This is a moment of glory and it will be the greatest moment of your entire life.

We drove on for a while longer in silence. I had the sensation of slipping under the surface of a liquid. As if I was sliding into an enveloping oil, sucking me under. I would be safe there.

— To do that, to become a hero and to save the world, you will have to join our group. Do you know what that means?

— No.

— But you are prepared to do it anyway, whatever it involves, whatever it takes?

I hesitated. She slammed on the brakes and the car screeched to a halt. I had not noticed before, but we were on a busy motorway. It was raining hard. I turned around, and through the refraction of a billion raindrops, I saw a wall of lights bearing down on us, heading towards us inexorably. I started to panic, the sweat pouring from my brow. I turned to her, wild with fear.

— What are you doing?

— Will you do it?

— We're going to die.

— Will you do it?

I turned back to the window. The lights were closer, closer, closer. I could hear the roar of the engines approaching, the first blasts on the horns as the drivers bearing down on us saw we were not moving.

— We're going to be killed. It… it…

— WILL YOU DO IT?

— WHAT?

— ANYTHING, TO JOIN US.

— YES, YES, ANYTHING, YES, JUST START DRIVING.

She slammed the car into gear and it lurched forward just before a truck, with its horn blaring and its lights filling the car with a horrible rain-refracted glare, hit the back of us. I stared out of the back window as we accelerated away from the metal grill and saw the panicked face of the driver, before he was lost in the spray.

I stared at her. She was calm, smiling even, not a bead of sweat on her brow, nothing but perfect beautiful curves arching into the perfect tumbling curls of the hair across her eyes. I had no idea what it all meant, what had happened.

All I knew was I was afraid of her.

I saw now she was capable of anything, that she was stronger and more determined and more reckless than I could ever be. I was afraid of that, and of what would happen to me. I knew there was no way out, and was unsure if I wanted to find a way out, even if I could.

But above all, finally my life had meaning.

I was alive.

For the first time.

· · ·

OBVIOUSLY THAT IS JUST a figure of speech. I have been alive ever since I was born. But you knew I would point that out, didn't you? After all we've been through up until this point? Of course I would. You didn't think you'd lost me, did you?

YOU HAD LOST ME. I had lost myself. I think it was the adrenaline rush from staring death in the face. Death had a chubby face, apparently, and stubble and, judging by the pictures in the back of his cab, had been to Rotterdam and liked busty women.

WE DIDN'T SAY anything for the rest of the journey. I stopped looking around and concentrated on being calm and obedient. I could see now she was in complete control, and I would do, without question, whatever she asked of me, whatever she told me to do.

As the time passed, my fear over what that meant dissipated and I decided I would accept the truth: she owned me now. The simplicity of that was comforting. No more decisions, just the dedication of my life to achieving her goals, following her leadership. There was something so beautiful in the clarity of that.

Maybe I would indeed become a hero, in the end. Maybe I would make a difference. Maybe I could help to save the world.

TWENTY-FIVE

I woke up as the car was drawing to a halt outside a ramshackle mansion in the middle of a wood. We must have left the main roads quite a while before, as the house was at the end of a dirt track and the darkness was profound and all-encompassing.

As the car stopped, she sat back and turned to look at me properly for the first time since I got in.

— Here we are. Your new home. From here, we, all of us, will help to save the world.

I looked at her and then again at the house, which was thrown into hard shadows and broken light by the headlamps.

She got out of the car and I followed a few paces behind. At the front door, which was at once imposing and impressive, she stopped and turned to me.

— You should be very proud of yourself. Few people in this world get the opportunity to do what you are about to do. You are special, and your life will be dedicated to the greatest cause that there can be: the salvation of humankind. You are to become the closest thing to a deity that is possible on this earth. Treasure this moment, and every moment you spend here.

She opened the door and walked in without looking back. I followed her and carefully closed the door behind me.

Inside, we entered a large space that may once have been a drawing room. There were ten or fifteen identical-looking people sitting around on the floor, on broken sofas, old chairs and dirty ripped bean bags, or standing, leaning against the old oak-panelled walls. Everyone's head was shaved and everyone was wearing the same grey jumpsuit and worker boots in rough, worn leather. In contrast to their anonymous uniformity, she looked magnificent, like a god among her disciples. Everyone gazed at her with reverence, and then looked at me, inspecting me, picking me apart.

I didn't know what I was supposed to do. She addressed the identical people, giving them information about things that made no sense to me. I watched her, lost in admiration. Once she had finished, she turned to me.

— Give me your wallet.

I took it out of my pocket and handed it over.

— Tell me your PIN.

I glanced around the room nervously.

— They have all done the same. Tell me.

I told her. (Isn't it strange that, even now, I still feel uncomfortable with the idea of sharing it, though that number has no relevance to you and even less to me.)

— Good. She nodded to one of the identical people. — Get him ready.

— What do you mean? I asked.

She smiled at me pityingly.

— Haven't you worked it out yet? Your hair will be shaved off, like everyone else's. She gestured around the room. — You will be given new clothes, like everyone else. You will be assigned a bunk in a dorm, like everyone else. And you will stop using your name and be given a number. Like everyone else.

I must have looked upset, or as if I might run away.

— You said you would do anything, she snapped.

— Yes, of course.

I lowered my eyes.

— Of course, Master, she corrected.

I looked up at her in surprise.

— Say it.

— Of course, Master.

The identical person she had nodded to before got up, took my hand. I looked into his eyes. They were kind and gentle. And then he led me out of the room.

THE NEXT MORNING, after a night of terrible dreams, I woke up scared and lonely. My head was cold from my lack of hair and the rough bedclothes itched. Somewhere, a gong had sounded and everyone was rushing around. I'd had no idea what I was supposed to do or where to go.

I realised everyone was quickly dressing and making their beds before running out of the dorm and downstairs. I jumped out of bed and pulled on my grey jumpsuit and boots, tidied up my bed as well as I could and ran after the last person, catching up with them as they left. Everyone was walking in single file, with their heads down, so I followed suit.

As we descended the stairs, I noticed the house was smaller than it had seemed the night before. All the shadows were now filled out with light and made ordinary. The paper on the walls was peeling in places and the carpet running down the middle of the stairs was threadbare and worn through.

At the bottom of the stairs, we turned the opposite way

from the room I had been in for my presentation the night before, and headed down a corridor that ran to the back of the house. At the end, we turned and entered a large room. I stopped and let my train of identical people carry on while I took it all in.

THEY DO THAT, in movies. The main character stops and takes in the scene while the rest of the people they were following carry on. It's for the benefit of the audience, to give them time to locate themselves. Here, you are the audience, whoever you may be.

THE ROOM WAS A HUGE, high-ceilinged kitchen, with sinks and stoves and cupboards full of cooking equipment down one side, and benches and tables down the other.

People, all of them identical, sat and ate or milled about. All silent, all with heads bowed. The sight itself wasn't so shocking or surprising. I had seen it a thousand times before in any number of films or television series. Although it may well be that my recollection of the scene, which appears to be a combination of *Oliver Twist*, the 1984 Apple Super Bowl Advert and the *Shawshank Redemption*, is less than perfect.

Maybe their heads weren't bowed. Maybe not everyone was wearing a grey jumpsuit. Another memory from that time has someone, who is definitely one of us, dressed in a dirty white t-shirt and jeans, looking like James Dean. He is mocking me in that other memory. I don't remember what everyone else was wearing then, or even me.

Does all of that matter? Perhaps it does if I am to give you a sense of verisimilitude.

Let's keep it simple. Let's say everyone was dressed in grey jumpsuits, with shaved heads bowed, identical souls shuffling around in our own circle of hell, waiting for what, we did not know. To imagine the scene like that would give you a proper sense of the mood, which was sombre, cold and forbidding.

I took some food, grey no doubt, and sat down at one of the benches. I tried to catch the eye of the identical person sitting next to me. I wanted to talk, to connect, to understand, to not be so alone.

No response.

I tried to speak, to interact and start a conversation, but I was ignored. I had a glance shot at me from someone on the other side of the table. Piercing angry eyes flashing from a tired and worn face. The eyes were no older than mine but they were weary, exhausted. There were tan lines on the side of his face but he wore no glasses. There was a pale stripe around his ring finger but no ring. His soft hands were marked with blisters and his skin was raw.

I bowed my head and ate up my grey food. Glancing up at the identical person on the other side of me, I inspected their face. I was feeling bold, reckless. They could see I was staring, but did not take the hint. Head bowed, they ate their food.

The man who had shot me a piercing stare got up and took his tray to the stand on the other side of the room. But now he was a woman. How had I not seen that before? Maybe in the loose jumpsuit, with her shaved head and her tired eyes, she had seemed like a man. But maybe I am mistaken.

Now, as I am typing this, I realise it either wasn't the same person as the one who gave me the piercing stare or I transformed her into a woman for this part of my memory because I wanted her to a woman. Or maybe I thought she was a woman because the next part of the memory has bled into this one, and the young man deprived of his glasses and wedding ring, who had his soft hands forced into manual work even though he was unsuitable for it, has become lost in the jumble of recollections.

WHAT BLED? Me. I bled. My heart bled. Gushing torrents. Because *she* walked into the room. She strode across the room in her high boots, purposeful, powerful, pulling us all into her, a maelstrom in our minds. She strode and everything stopped. I forgot about the man/woman; I forgot about the grey food; I forgot about being scared.

I looked up to her, searched her face, pleaded, begged for her to see me, to recognise me, to give me something, anything. But she ignored me. She ignored everyone, even though everyone had stopped and was staring at her; even though everyone had straightened and stood to attention.

She strode on across the room and left by the other door, and I was alone again. Colder and more alone than I had ever been. I was empty.

I DIDN'T KNOW what to do all day. There was nothing to do, or no one gave me anything to do. I wandered around, looking in different rooms, trying to speak to people, trying to catch their eye, trying to help. It was frustrating. I just wanted someone to acknowledge me. Maybe I was invisible. Identical and invisible.

I wandered around again, then sat down outside. I sat on an old tree stump and looked at the house, wondering about its age and how she came to take it over. Then I saw her again. She was outside, walking away from the house, in my direction. She was walking towards me. My heart racing, I stood up, smoothing down my jumpsuit and smiling. Maybe she saw me, maybe she didn't, but either way, she turned away from me and walked around the other side of the house.

I stood and watched her disappear, crushed.

THE NEXT TIME I saw her, she was inside the house, on the phone by a downstairs window, talking calmly, although I couldn't hear what she was saying. I was close by, on the other side of the window; I caught her eye and waved. She dismissed me with a flick of her wrist.

I was elated. She had seen me, she had acknowledged my presence. At least she knew I was there for her.

THEN I SAW SOMETHING. Was it that day, or another? They all merge into one. I don't know how long it was after I arrived. Maybe only a few days, but it could have been several weeks.

The days were almost identical. We would wake early, go downstairs and have breakfast, and then we were supposed to do things for the mission.

The evening of my first full day there, after a dinner of the same grey food we'd had for breakfast, she gave another pep talk, as she had done when I had arrived. It became clear she was issuing instructions and giving us updates on things we were meant to get ready so we could launch the fightback against the dark forces and save the human race.

Each evening, she would tell us how the dark forces were replacing more and more people with androids, and we must step up our efforts. She and her spies were gathering knowledge on how the dark forces were operating, and she was sure we could make a definitive strike against them in the coming weeks.

She would give commands, and then pick someone to carry them out, often choosing someone who appeared unsuited for the task. At first, I was given only the smallest and most menial tasks, such as cleaning the toilets or working in the kitchen, but then I was given more complex jobs, some even related to the mission.

Still no one would talk to me, so I had to do everything by copying others or working it out for myself.

It was good for me to be doing physical work, and at first I started to feel much better and less worried. I slept well in that quiet house in the middle of the woods, and my dreams were less frightening and traumatic.

And then I saw something.

It was in the woods. I wasn't in the woods; I was fetching wood for the fire, but I looked up and saw someone walking quickly through the trees near the house. He was dressed in white, or he was in my recollection of it, and he looked straight ahead as he walked.

Shivers ran down my spine and I froze. He walked on, through the trees, and I turned away with tears in my eyes. Had *he* always been there, waiting for me, after all these years? Was this why I was supposed to go there? To see him again?

AND THEN IT HAPPENED AGAIN. Two days later. I wasn't fetching wood this time; I don't remember what I was doing, but I was in front of the house, gazing at the line of trees and the dark shadows beyond.

A flash of white, and then nothing.

And then there he was, my friend who had died, walking through the woods, purposefully, turning away from my direction. I called out to him. I ran into the trees, even though I heard someone call after me, and tried to catch up with him.

He was always too far ahead of me, just out of reach,

always turning away as I was arriving. But I knew it *was* him. No doubt. If only I could catch up with him, maybe I could get to speak to him again, hear his voice again, after all this time.

I tripped and fell. I don't know how far I was from the house, but I was in a dark space between the trees. He was no longer there and the air was cold. I didn't know where I was, or how I would get back.

There was rustling in the trees, a faint breeze, and I heard her. Her voice, calling out, drifting across the cool air.

I sensed something behind me and turned to find the magnificent parrot standing over me, her iridescent black feathers rustling and her glass dark eyes staring at me. I was afraid of what she would do to me. I scrabbled backwards and she moved towards me. I tumbled over a branch and she lunged for me, her dark, hooked beak jabbing at me.

I managed to scramble free and ran, I don't know where. I could hear her flying just behind me, her dark wings beating in the cool air. I dared not turn back. Night was falling, and I stumbled and pushed my way through the branches and the trees, heading towards a light in the distance, always sensing her close to me.

On and on and on I ran, even though I could no longer hear her. I still dared not turn back. I was too afraid. So I ran on and on, tripping and falling, pulling myself up, forcing myself to continue, ignoring the cuts and the pain, until eventually I burst through the trees and found myself back in front of the house, exactly where I had left all that time ago.

My grey jumpsuit was dirty and bedraggled, and I was tired and thirsty. I didn't know if dinner was over, and I trudged my way to the kitchen, passing identical people who stared in amazement at my appearance, but said nothing.

I managed to get some grey food, and later that evening I went to the room where I had been taken on the first night, where all heads were silent and bowed. As always, identical people sat on the floor, on broken sofas, old chairs and sprawled on dirty bean bags. I don't know if they were the same people who I'd seen on the first night. I do not really know how many people were staying there.

I HAVE BEEN ASKED, during various conversations, whether the atmosphere there was similar to that in the place where I had spent the previous few months, before she picked me up at the gate. *They* asked whether I had a sense of familiarity, or even safety, while I was there.

At the previous place, there was of course clarity and light, whereas here there was none. At the other place, the aim was to care for me, for us, whereas here the aim was somehow elusive, even though the stated objective was extremely clear. At the other place, I could not leave when I wanted, but I felt protected, secure. Here, I could theoretically leave whenever I wanted and take my chances in the woods, but I was neither protected nor safe.

I SAT down in the same place as always, near a group of people who I assumed were always the same. But I had learned my lesson. I no longer tried to catch anyone's eye or speak to them.

— Do you want some weed? a voice whispered next to my ear.

— What? I said, shocked. I tried to turn around, amazed and delighted to have been spoken to, and puzzled as to which one of the identical people could have finally opened his mouth (this one was definitely a he).

— Don't turn around, he hissed. — Don't look at me. You will never know my face.

— Okay.

— Well, do you want some?

— No, thank you. I don't really like it, and my doctor told me I should be careful as it might disturb my mind.

— But there is nothing wrong with you, a voice boomed out.

She, the magnificent she, strode into the room and pointed straight at me. The room fell instantly silent and I panicked.

— There is nothing wrong with you, is there?

I didn't know what to say. My mind was frozen.

— We both know that.

She dropped her hand and stood with her feet apart, staring straight at me. I could see out of the corner of my eye that, one by one, all of the identical people were turning to look at me. I wanted to look away but I was transfixed by her and the light that glowed from within.

— I knew that the first time I set eyes on you, right from the first moment I heard your voice on the telephone. I knew it when I stood outside that metal gate, waiting to take you away, and when I drove you here. I knew it then and I know it now. There is nothing wrong with you. You never needed those medications and you do not need to worry about your mind. It is *they* who are wrong. *They* are the ones who misunderstood you and tried to put you into a box and shut you away from the world, from yourself.

She said that last word almost in a whisper and I wanted so much to believe her.

— I could tell a similar story about every one of you in this room, she said, sweeping her arm around the room. — Each one of you, misunderstood and maltreated, not believed and marginalised by a society that did not want to know. And for what? All because you had discovered the truth. A truth we, individually and together, have found and they want to hide from us, to stop us telling the world. They want to drug us and shut us away, to silence our mouths and blind our eyes, to pretend none of it is happening or, worse, because they are one of them. Only here are you safe, only here do you know for sure there are no androids, only here are there no dark forces, only here is no one to stop us rising up and saving humanity, and only here will you always be told the truth.

She paused and looked around the room.

— Next week. She nodded her head and smiled. — Yes, that's right. Next week, our plans will come to fruition and we will begin the fightback. Our stock piles are almost complete and we can launch the revolution against the androids, against the dark forces, against anyone who tries to stop us.

Everyone in the room cheered and raised their fists in anticipated triumph. I followed them, raising my hand, cheering quietly, and looked around the room.

And there she was. My stomach dropped and my heart stopped. The breath caught in my throat. There she was, Lucy, her mouth open in a broad smile, gazing out across the room, her face lit up with joy. Lucy. My Lucy.

— Are you all right?

A hand was on my arm, a woman's hand, with fingers thin and light, and I looked up to smile at her and tell her everything is okay, but she had no face. I looked around, panicking, searching the room for something, anything, but not one of the people there had a face.

I turned to her, the magnificent she, pleading with my eyes, begging.

— Helen, I called out in desperation.

She glared at me as if I had made the worst mistake of my life and strode out of the room.

TWENTY-SIX

In the middle of the night, when the darkness had not yet given way to light, I woke. I didn't know why at first, but then I could feel a knee pushing apart my thighs and a body clambering on top of mine. My arms were pinned down. Clumsy, fumbling.

I was frightened initially, but then I just wanted them off me. They clambered and pushed, forcing my legs apart and putting their entire body weight on my arms.

— What are you…

I tried to speak, but then a mouth, stinking of rancid alcohol and stale cigarette smoke, was on mine and a tongue was pushing its way around my teeth, then connecting with my tongue. Metallic tasting saliva slid into my mouth. I opened my eyes and tried to work out who it was, but I could see only their bright eyes shining in the darkness.

While I was struggling, a knee pressed heavily against my left arm and a hand reached down and started kneading my penis. I pulled my right hand free and tried to push against their chest, but it was made difficult by the weight of their head holding mine down, pressing me into the pillow.

I could not turn, and could barely breathe, while their tongue roughly explored my mouth and our teeth clashed. Their drunkenness made them heavy, floppy, unwieldy, but I managed eventually to twist and turn enough to hook a leg between theirs and flip them straight off the bed and on to the floor.

They crashed heavily on their back and I leapt out of bed, initially standing there panting. A light came on, then the main light of the dorm. Identical people got out of bed and asked what was going on.

Before I could say anything or turn around, she strode in and stood there in the middle of the room, her feet apart and her hands on her hips.

— What on earth is going on here?

I was beyond relieved to see her. I think I may have actually sighed.

— Well?

— Someone tried to rape me, Master, I said, more clearly than I had ever said anything before.

She arched an eyebrow. — Oh really, she sneered.

— Yes, it was this person here.

I turned and pointed to the floor next to my bed. But I don't have to tell you there was no one there, do I? When did you work it out? As soon as the light came on? When she strode into the room?

It was obvious, inevitable, even. We've seen it a thousand times before in a thousand stories. And sure enough, the space on the ground I pointed to was empty, with no sign of anyone having been there.

Of course, I played my part in this well-worn drama and protested there had been someone there. Someone had tried to force themselves on me, and why would I lie about a thing like that, etc, etc. She played her part and said I was making it all up, I was a trouble-maker, I needed to learn a lesson, I wouldn't be allowed to get away with disturbing the unity of the group, let alone the success of the mission. She couldn't let that happen, not now they had come this far, etc, etc.

So far, so predictable. I suppose there should be no prizes for guessing what happened next. Have you worked it out yet? Yes, that's right. She demonstrated her absolute power over me by ordering the identical people to drag me out of the room and down the stairs, and I saw the cruel hatred in their eyes, and I knew it was all over.

IT WAS ONLY LATER, much later, it occurred to me they had set me up. It had all seemed a little too convenient, a little contrived, almost.

Later. There was a lot of later to have all sorts of thoughts in.

THE IDENTICAL PEOPLE dragged me downstairs and then through a door I hadn't noticed next to the kitchen, down another flight of stairs and into a dank basement.

It was the man with the tan lines on his face and the missing ring who hit me first. I recognised his hands, even when bunched into fists. But I didn't try to recognise anyone else. I let them do what they needed to do. They were angry and I was their outlet. I think I understood why they were angry with me.

She hadn't told them to hit me, but she hadn't needed to. She knew they were frustrated and reduced, and would take any opportunity to exact revenge on someone perceived to be weaker than them. Especially if to do so came with tacit approval.

Fortunately, they were not skilled fighters, particularly fit, nor possessing of what might be called the killer instinct.

They shied away from any truly serious blows, although I was in pain. After a while, they stood back and stared at me on the floor, still and motionless while they panted, unsatisfied but unable to do more.

When they lifted me up and dumped me in a chair, I realised I had at least one cracked rib and my face was badly bruised. Someone must have stood on my ankle at some point, as it was weak and loose, and shards of pain pushed into my leg every time it moved.

They tied and gagged me, then left without looking back. They turned out the lights and slammed the door at the top of the stairs before locking it.

I heard footsteps, muffled voices and the scratching of rats. And the darkness lay heavily over my eyes.

I WOKE up when they opened the door. They brought me grey food and some water, and a clean bucket. Each time they came, it was a different identical person. I suppose I served as a lesson to them all.

During these visits, I inspected the identical people, my jailers, and I saw they were not identical after all. Some were women, and some were men; some tall and some not. Some older and some younger. And they were of different races. But they all had something in common. They had empty, absent eyes, and a fear that lingered in everything they did.

Was I like that?

FOOTSTEPS, muffled voices and the scratching of rats. Those were the markers that laid out the days, alongside the rumble of the occasional coming and going of vehicles. There was no light down there, only sounds and smells. The sound of movement and the smell of decay.

I had thought I might be able to escape, but I knew that, alone, I would be found and captured. And I was afraid I might see the man in white walking through the woods. I thought I saw him, in fact, as I drifted between sleep and wakefulness in the infinite darkness. And he *was* there, fleetingly, in the corner of the room.

I saw his face and I cried.

I cried into my gag. It was wet with saliva and perspiration, and dirty from the soil that fell in a soft rain from the ceiling as people walked overhead.

AND THEN SHE APPEARED. I woke up, groggy and in pain. The light was on, and there she stood, her hands on her hips and feet apart, smiling at me sardonically. The perfect curls of her dark hair hanging down over her perfect hard eyes and the porcelain of her skin.

A statue. An idol. A totem.

— Helen, I croaked.

She laughed.

— You never did understand.

— What do you mean?

She leaned forward, close to my face. I could almost sense her perfect breath on my skin.

— You never understood what this is all about, did you? And now it's too late.

I screwed up my eyes, and the tears flowed. I sobbed.

I heard her stand up, her clothes rustling as she moved. I opened my eyes to plead with her. But she was not there. The magnificent parrot was standing in her stead, her iridescent blank feathers shimmering in the weak light of the lamp hanging down from the ceiling.

— Who are you? I whispered.

She tilted her head and opened her beak, and slowly

transformed into a snake. She slithered her way over to me. I tried to pull back in my chair, but it was no use. I was tied down and there was no escape.

She slithered up my leg and, as she reached my dirty, stained hand, she opened her mouth and enveloped my fingers. I screamed out in agony and tried to pull my hand free. But it was too late; her fangs were already deep into my skin, pumping venomous fluid into me.

I could see them, my veins, stained black as the venom coursed up inside me, poisoning my arm. I became weak and I knew I was near the end. She thrashed about in excitement as she saw me succumb, and I called out one last time, my voice weak, for someone, anyone to help me.

And there, from the shadows, she came. Shimmering white, her kind and gentle beak tilted towards me, her eyes glass bright and shining. The magnificent dove. The snake couldn't pull free in time. One touch of her perfect white wing was enough.

And then she was there beside me, her beak close to my mouth, and I knew I would live.

TWENTY-SEVEN

WHAT IS SILENCE? IT IS THE ABSENCE OF NOISE, ONE WOULD say. And yet there is rarely absolute silence. Wherever we are, there are the sounds of other people or animals or the creak of a house or the rustle of the trees. In the city, that gets lost in the hum, the throb, the endless vibration of the traffic, the machines, the electricity, penetrating and subduing. In the countryside, the sounds may be different, less insistent, but they are there nonetheless.

No, silence is not the absence of noise; it is a notable absence of an expected noise, the implication that its absence came about all of a sudden. Silence can come over a room, a group of people, a place.

There, in that basement, it was all three at once.

I was awake. I assumed it was night-time at first, as there were no footsteps, no muffled voices, not even the hint of a car or truck. And yet it couldn't be night as there was no scratching from the rats.

It was the absence of light during the daytime that made me think it was night.

I listened hard, I strained, I pulled against my ropes. My

jumpsuit was wet and warm. I must have urinated on myself in my sleep. I listened again.

Nothing. Silence. Or the absence of an expected sound.

And then it struck me. The house was empty. Without people, even those who are sleeping, a house becomes a carcass, a shell divided into compartments, a pile of bricks and dead eyes staring out.

I WAITED a while before I thought about getting out of my bonds and going upstairs. I did not want to take any risks, and after all this time, I no longer fully trusted myself.

Then I became impatient to leave my prison. With sore and cracked hands, I pulled and tugged at the rough rope until it loosened and my arms could hang free. What relief, what joy. For a while, I simply sat there, my blood circulating, rotating my shoulders from time to time, shoulders now weak and bony.

It seems strange to admit that it took a few moments for me to remember I had the gag in my mouth and pull it off to breathe deeply the stale, humid air.

I quickly untied my feet and tried to stand up, but my ankle gave way and the pain doubled me up. I knelt, and then sat on the earthen floor for a while, letting the pain subside and thinking about what I should do next.

Using the chair, I pulled myself back up, and then hobbled over to the stairs, half-dragging myself up them, hand over hand, step by step.

The door was locked. I hadn't thought of that. And it opened inwards. I hadn't thought of that either. I tugged and tugged at the door handle and nearly fell down the stairs before I noticed the key hanging on a hook by the door.

. . .

THE SUNLIGHT WAS BLINDING. I had to crouch on the floor, my eyes screwed tight shut, my arm over them, waiting for them to adjust. My lids were sticky with dust and dirt, and once I was able, I pulled myself over to the sink in the kitchen and washed my face again and again until it was clean. All the while, I expected someone to appear, her perhaps, but the house was completely empty.

I stumbled around, unsure what I was expecting to find. I had thought the house might be like the *Mary Celeste*, abandoned at a moment's notice, with plates and cutlery left on the tables, and belongings dropped in a hurry. But there was nothing, not a trace of anyone having lived there in maybe twenty years. All the old, broken furniture was gone. There was nothing there. I even searched upstairs, but that may have been because I was afraid to go through the woods and out into the world.

I STOOD at the window in one of the upstairs rooms and looked out over the clearing in front of the house. It was a bright, beautiful day. I imagined, if the window had been open, I might have heard the birds singing.

But there was only silence, or the absence of an expected noise.

TWENTY-EIGHT

It took several hours to get to the nearest town. I walked all the way. Trudged, really. I was so weak and hungry, although my ankle became less painful the more I walked. I didn't try to get a lift. I knew no one would take me.

And then, there it was. Normality. Normal lives, normal people, normal concerns and normal cares. But I was not normal. I was in a dirty, urine-stained grey jumpsuit, with a shaved head growing out, and I didn't dare even look in a shop window to see what state my face was in. I rubbed my chin. I had grown something resembling a beard, although the hair was thin and straggly.

I didn't know where I was, nor where I had come from. I was in a small market town, that much was obvious. I wanted to talk to someone, to hear their accent, their voice and to ask... well, everything. But no one would let me close. They turned away, they batted me away with their hands, they shunned me, they even shouted at me and flung obscenities.

— We don't want your sort here.

What was that, exactly? My sort?

They treated me like I wasn't a human being.

And after all I had been through to help save humanity. Typical.

I WANDERED AIMLESSLY FOR A WHILE, before turning a corner to find a policeman walking towards me. I thought of running, but realised I couldn't, and then it struck me I needed his help. As he approached, I fell apart.

— I want to go home, I pleaded.

— And where would that be?

I stared at him, my mind completely blank.

— Do you have any form of ID?

Tears welled up. — They took it from me. They took everything from me.

— It's okay. Don't worry. Why don't you come with me?

The policeman firmly but gently hooked his slab hand into my elbow and led me to his car. They stared at me, the people on the street. I saw their judgement and I guessed the narrative playing in their heads. I wanted to shout 'It's not what you think', but maybe it was.

AT THE POLICE STATION, they asked me my name. I could remember that. After a cup of tea and a biscuit, I could remember a little more and they told me I was a missing person. I wondered how I could have been reported missing. By whom?

By my boss, apparently. It hurt a little to know that was how I had been missed, and a little more to know I had let him down. Again.

They asked me what happened, and I told them, from when I walked through the gates with the clarity and light and got into her car for the first time. I mean the facts of what happened. How I ended up in that house in the woods and what they were planning there.

But you and I both know it wasn't that simple.

There were two of me in that interview room, you see. The one that wanted so badly to tell someone, anyone, everything that had happened to me; who wanted so desperately some human contact, some connection, to no longer feel alone and to get everything off his chest, to plead, to beg for help, any help, and to feel safe. He would have gone through anything, said anything, just to unburden himself and know it will all, please, stop.

Then there was the other me, the one that knew my words would have an effect; that if I said certain things, there was a possibility I would never get home again. He was a much more calculating me, who had a modicum of pride left in him and wanted to believe I could resume my normal life.

But did I really want to? Go home, I mean. What was waiting there for me? What would happen to me if I did?

— I want to go home.

— I'm afraid I've got some bad news.

That was when I knew it was all over.

I would like to recount some grand, fantastical vision of how the world collapsed around me. Maybe I should tell you the policeman became a dove and flew out of the window, or I struck up a conversation with a loquacious chair and she showed me a secret door that led back to the city. You know me well enough by now to expect something like that. But it was all so much more prosaic.

I'VE OFTEN THOUGHT of that moment, and I'm thinking of it now as I type.

It's a nice day today, sunny and warm. I took a walk

earlier, because the typewriter wasn't free, and I thought I could do with spending some time in the garden. I walked down to the trees and watched the river run through the leaves. The sun was on my back and I was warm and content.

We watched a Doris Day musical last night. The one where she is a tomboy mechanic and her young man comes back from the war and wants to put off getting married until he has enough money. She is mighty disappointed and they have such fights, and she shows she can give as good as she gets. But, you know, they work it out in the end and true love prevails.

I hadn't seen that one. I think it's called *By the Light of the Silvery Moon*. It's not my favourite. I liked *April in Paris* a lot. But it warmed me in its kitsch way all the same, just as the sun did this morning.

But despite all that warmth, I was not exactly happy. You see, I was itching to be at the typewriter. The man who was using it this morning, he waved at me through the window when he had finished. He's not normally like that. Maybe the Doris Day movie had warmed him too.

So I was in a good mood, if not exactly happy, when I sat down to type. And then I remembered how I felt when the policeman told me he was afraid he had some bad news.

THE STRANGEST THING happened when those words fell out of his mouth. I became aware, hyperaware, of everything. The texture of the Formica table, the whiteness of its surface, the hum of the air conditioning, the reflection on the lens of the CCTV camera in the corner of the ceiling, the slight clubbing of the policeman's yellow-stained fingers, the way his neck spilled over the collar of his shirt, the scrape of my leather boot on the floor, and even the breath in my throat.

I vomited when he told me my apartment had been repossessed and sold for non-payment of the mortgage.

— But now long have I been away? I asked in a hoarse whisper.

A year, it turned out. My bank accounts had been frozen after I systematically, every day, withdrew as much money as I could on my cards until they were empty.

I say 'I', but I mean 'she', of course.

My company had stopped paying me, and so there was no money for my mortgage. After I was reported as a missing person and there was no trace of me, the bank had no choice but to sell the flat to recoup their money, and my belongings, such that had any value, were sold at auction.

I had nothing. There was nothing left of my life. Everything was gone.

I thought about my coffee machine and the bed I had spent so much money on. And the view from my apartment across the river. I had been so happy when I bought that place.

But I hadn't been that happy for a long while.

As for 'them', the identical people, there was no trace. Nowhere. But you'd guessed that, right? There had been no revolution. Not yet, anyway. And the police couldn't find her. She had disappeared. No one matching her description turned up at all. It didn't help that I wasn't sure of her name.

I didn't mention the snake.

And I didn't talk about dark forces and androids and the end of human life as we know it, or how I ended up in the place I was staying in when she came to fetch me. The place with the clarity and the light.

Once they saw I had been in that place, for several months, the policeman made some assumptions about me I didn't have the strength to argue with. I should have tried to make him see I was so much more than that.

But maybe I wasn't, in the end.

I was just so tired, you see. I needed some rest.

AND SO WE kept coming back to the same thing.

— I have nowhere to go.

— It would seem that way, unless you have any family you can go to.

I had a sister, for one day.

— No, no one. And I have no money.

The policeman nodded.

— And I have no job, either. I don't really exist anymore, do I?

— Sort of, but you can exist again, if you believe in yourself. If you truly believe, you can do anything.

He didn't say that, surely. He can't have, can he? I have my doubts. He was a middle-aged man who lived a quiet life as a policeman in a quiet market town in the countryside. I don't think he would have had much truck with fancy talk, as my father might have said.

But it sounds like a nice thing to say. And he was a nice man, a kind man. He wanted to reassure me, to make me feel like all was not lost. He didn't want me to... what? Fall any further down the hole, I suppose is a good way of putting it.

WHEN THEY TOOK me away from the police station and brought me to the place I'm in now, with the typewriter and the garden where the rivers of air flow through the line of trees, I think I was relieved.

Of course, I hadn't wanted things to turn out this way. I would have liked to have been able to go back to my apartment with the view of the river, and to my job, and maybe start travelling again. But I knew I wasn't capable. Not then. Maybe never.

And everyone was so very kind.

THEY TOLD me to write this, these recollections, by the way.

Not straight away, of course. We had some getting-to-know-you time when I arrived, but after a while, they suggested it might be a good idea to put everything down on paper, to recount my story. They said it should help to work it all out in my head, and maybe to fill in some blanks.

It became a lot easier to write after I read about her in a magazine I found in the common room. I didn't recognise the name she was using, but the perfect curls of her hair hanging down over her perfect porcelain skin gave her away.

I learned she had been arrested and put away for being a serial con artist. It turns out persuading vulnerable people to join a cult and part with all their money was the favourite of her tricks. Quite the Svengali, apparently. It didn't make me feel any more special to know that, but at least I knew I hadn't made it all up.

WE, *they* and I, have talked about what I've written in these pages. Some things we've talked about a lot. You see, I show them each section I've written the next time we sit down together, so we can discuss it.

It was they who suggested this whole thing, everything that happened to me, might be due to suppressed memories. The seeing of people from my past, I mean. People, by whom I mean two in particular: Lucy and him.

It wasn't easy to accept, when they implied that was the root of it all. I should have seen it coming, of course, but my stomach fell away from me all the same. I stared at them for a long time when they brought it up. I think my face must have crumpled because they asked me whether I had ever talked about it before, about how I felt about it.

A tear rolled down my face. That surprised me because... there is no because. A tear rolled down my face, and I was there again, driving through the night, Lucy in the passenger seat and him in the back. We were on our way back from a friend's wedding. We'd had so much fun. It was always special being with those two, but that night, with the beauty and love of the married couple and the lights and the dancing and everyone in high spirits, I was transported.

Like in a Doris Day movie.

I WAS in one of my non-drinking periods. They breathalysed me twice afterwards and took my blood just to make sure. And they held me overnight in a police cell. They took away my belt and my laces and I cried and cried and cried, scratching the floor and the walls, anything to get to them, anything to bring them back.

I'd only turned away for a second, to laugh at a joke he had made. We all laughed and I loved watching Lucy being happy. She was always so radiant in those moments. Okay, it was a right-hand corner and I should have been paying more attention, but who would have expected a truck to be on the wrong side of the road in the middle of the night?

He confessed, in the end. The truck driver. The police apologised and everything was quietly dropped. But I was left to twist on the rope all the same, dangling in mid-air. I see now I was never the same again.

. . .

SURVIVOR GUILT. *They* called it that, too. I guess I had tried not to think about that night ever again. I had tried to move on.

Tried.

Failed.

What I really did was run away from my feelings and bury them under work and travel, and drown them in alcohol.

I see now it had all been festering underneath the surface for many years. I guess by the time I ended up in the queue in the Japanese restaurant, I was a bit too run down, a bit too close to the edge, a bit too far gone to hold it all back.

But I hadn't noticed I was in that state. You never do when things happen bit by bit, day by day. Further and further out you go past the edge, not realising how far you will fall until you see how high up you are.

I NEVER COULD DO ENOUGH to make up for it, for the pain I had caused. I had no one to go to, no one to hold me when I cried. Their parents blamed me. They said it was all my fault.

His parents, the parents of my friend who died, took out a private prosecution against me, even though the truck driver had said it was his fault. They claimed I was negligent because I didn't insist their boy wear a seatbelt. They lost the case, but it broke me all the more. I don't blame them for pouring all their guilt and hurt on to me. I would have done the same.

I did do the same.

HE CAME out of the woods to see me, you know. It was a couple of weeks ago, after I wrote about my arrest at the conference. He was dressed in white, like he was when I saw him in the trees near the house. I don't know why, he never wore white in real life. Maybe it's another culturally received idea. I think I've watched too many films and now I don't have an original thought in my head.

Anyway, there he was, and we talked. He told me Lucy is okay and still smiling, still laughing. I cried. He told me it's okay, it doesn't matter anymore. He reached out to console me, and I tried to put my hand in his, but it wasn't there.

ABOUT THE AUTHOR

L. A. Davenport is an Anglo-Irish author. He sometimes lives in the countryside, far away from urban distraction, but mostly he lives in the city. He enjoys long walks, typewriters and strong black coffee.

To find out when L. A. Davenport has a new book out and get the latest updates, visit his official website at Pushing the Wave. He can also be found on Twitter and Facebook.

ALSO BY L. A. DAVENPORT

FICTION

Escape

No Way Home

Dear Lucifer and Other Stories

NON-FICTION

My Life as a Dog

Printed in Great Britain
by Amazon